The *Circus*
of adventure

Enid Blyton, who died in 1968, is one of the most successful children's authors of all time. She wrote over seven hundred books, which have been translated into more than forty languages and have sold more than 400 million copies around the world. Enid Blyton's stories of magic, adventure and friendship continue to enchant children the world over. Enid Blyton's beloved works include The Famous Five, Malory Towers, The Faraway Tree and the Adventure series.

Titles in the Adventure series:

The *Circus*
of adventure

Enid Blyton™

MACMILLAN CHILDREN'S BOOKS

First published 1952 by Macmillan Children's Books

This edition published 2012 by Macmillan Children'sBooks
a division of Macmillan Publishers Limited
20 New Wharf Road, London N1 9RR
Basingstoke and Oxford
Associated companies throughout the world
www.panmacmillan.com

ISBN 978-1-4472-2063-3

3 5 7 9 8 6 4 2

A CIP catalogue record for this book is available from
the British Library.

Typeset by Intype Libra Ltd
Printed and bound in the UK by CPI Group (UK) Ltd, Croydon, CR0 4YY

Contents

1

Home from school

The quiet house was quiet no longer! The four children were back from boarding school, and were even now dragging in their trunks, shouting to one another. Kiki the parrot joined in the general excitement, of course, and screeched loudly.

'Aunt Allie! We're back!' yelled Jack. 'Be quiet, Kiki! I can't hear myself shout!'

'Mother! Where are you?' called Dinah. 'We're home again!'

Her mother appeared in a hurry, smiles all over her face. 'Dinah! Philip! I didn't expect you quite so soon. Well, Lucy-Ann, you've grown! And Philip, you look bursting with health!'

'I don't know why,' grinned Philip, giving Mrs Cunningham a big hug. 'The food at school is so frightful I never eat any of it!'

'Same old story!' said Mrs Cunningham, laughing. 'Hallo, Kiki! Say how do you do!'

'How do you do?' said the parrot, solemnly, and held out her left foot as if to shake hands.

'New trick,' said Jack. 'But wrong foot, old thing. Don't you know your left from your right yet?'

'Left, right, left, right, left, right,' said Kiki at once, and began marking time remarkably well. 'Left, right, left . . .'

'That's enough,' said Jack. He turned to Mrs Cunningham. 'How's Bill? Is he here too?'

'He meant to be here to welcome you all,' said Mrs Cunningham, Bill's wife. 'But he had a sudden 'phone call this morning, took the car, and went racing off to London all in a hurry.'

The four children groaned. 'It isn't some job that's turned up just as we're home for the Easter hols, is it?' said Lucy-Ann. 'Bill's always got some secret work to do just at the wrong time!'

'Well, I hope it isn't,' said Mrs Cunningham. 'I'm expecting him to telephone at any moment to say if he's going to be back tonight or not.'

'Mother! Shall we unpack down here and take our things up straight away?' called Dinah. 'Four trunks lying about the hall leave no room to move.'

'Yes. But leave two of the trunks downstairs when they're empty,' said her mother. 'We're going off on a holiday tomorrow, all of us together!'

This was news to the children. They clustered round Mrs Cunningham at once. 'You never said a word in your letters! Where are we going? Why didn't you tell us before?'

'Well, it was really Bill's idea, not mine,' said Mrs Cunningham. 'He just thought it would make a nice change. I was surprised myself when he arranged it.'

'Arranged it! And never said a word to us!' said Philip. 'I say – is anything up? It seems funny that Bill did it all of a sudden. Last time I saw him, when he came down to school to see us, he was talking about what we'd all do at *home* in the four weeks' Easter hols.'

'I don't really think there's anything *peculiar* about it,' said his mother. 'Bill gets these sudden ideas, you know.'

'Well – where are we all going to, then?' asked Jack, pushing Kiki off the sideboard, where she was trying to take the lid off the biscuit jar.

'It's a place called Little Brockleton,' said Mrs Cunningham. 'Very quiet. In the middle of the country. Just the kind of place you all like. You can mess about in old things all day long.'

'Little *Brock*leton,' said Philip. 'Brock means badger. I wonder if there are badgers there. I've always wanted to study badgers. Lovely little bear-like beasts.'

'Well, *you*'ll be happy then,' said Dinah. 'I suppose that means you'll be keeping a couple of badgers for pets before we know where we are! Ugh!'

'Badgers are very nice animals,' began Philip. 'Clean and most particular in their habits, and . . .'

Lucy-Ann gave a little squeal of laughter. 'Oh dear – they don't sound a *bit* like you then, Philip!'

'Don't interrupt like that and don't make silly remarks,' said Philip. 'I was saying, about badgers . . .'

But nobody wanted to listen. Jack had a question he wanted to ask. 'Are there any decent birds round about Little Brockleton?' he said. 'Where *is* it? By the sea?'

Jack was as mad as ever about birds. So long as he could do birdwatching of some kind he was happy. Mrs Cunningham laughed at him.

'You and your birds, Jack, and Philip and his badgers! I can't tell you anything about the birds there – the same ones as usual, I suppose. Now – what about these trunks? We'll unpack the lot; take the boys' trunks upstairs, and leave the girls' to take with us to Little Brockleton – they are not *quite* so hard-used as yours!'

'Can we have something to eat after we've unpacked?' asked Philip. 'I'm famished. The school food, you know, is so . . .'

'Yes – I've heard all that before, Philip,' said his mother. 'You'll have a fine lunch in half an hour – yes, your favourite – cold meat, salad, baked beans in tomato sauce, potatoes in their jackets, heaps of tomatoes . . .'

'Oh, good!' said everyone at once, and Kiki hopped solemnly from one leg to another.

'Good!' she said. 'Good! Good morning, good night, good!'

The unpacking began. 'Kiki was dreadful in the train

home,' said Jack, struggling with an armful of clothes, and dropping half of them. 'She got under the carriage seat to pick over some old toffee papers there, and such a nice old man got in. Kiki stuffed the toffee papers into the turn-ups of his trousers – you should just have seen his face when he bent down and saw them!'

'And then she began to bark like a dog,' said Lucy-Ann with a giggle, 'and the poor old man leapt off his seat as if he'd been shot.'

'Bang-bang,' put in Kiki. 'Pop-pop. Pop goes the weasel. Wipe your feet and shut the door.'

'Oh, Kiki! It's nice to have you again with your silly talk,' said Mrs Cunningham, laughing. Kiki put up her crest and sidled over to her. She rubbed her head against Mrs Cunningham's hand like a cat.

'I always expect you to purr, Kiki, when you do that,' said Mrs Cunningham, scratching the parrot's head.

The unpacking was soon done. It was very simple really. Dirty clothes were pitched into the enormous linen-basket, the rest were pitched into drawers.

'Can't think why people ever make a fuss about packing or unpacking,' said Jack. 'Kiki, take your head out of my pocket. What's this sudden craze for toffees? Do you want to get your beak stuck so that you can't talk?'

Kiki took her head out of Jack's pocket, and screeched triumphantly. She had found a toffee. Now she would have a perfectly lovely time unwrapping the paper, talking to herself all the while.

'Well, that'll keep her quiet for a bit,' said Dinah thankfully. 'Kiki's always so noisy when she's excited.'

'So are you,' said Philip at once. Dinah glared at him.

'Shut up, you two,' said Jack. 'No sparring on the first day of hols. Gosh, look at Lucy-Ann going up the stairs dropping a pair of socks on every step!'

The telephone bell rang. Mrs Cunningham ran to answer it. 'That will be Bill!' she said.

It was. There was a short conversation which consisted mostly of 'Yes. No. I see. I suppose so. No, of course not. Yes. Yes. No, Bill. Right. Yes, I'll explain. See you tonight then. Goodbye.'

'What's he say?' asked Lucy-Ann. 'Is he coming soon? I do want to see him.'

'Yes, he's coming this evening, about half past five,' said Mrs Cunningham. The four children didn't think she looked very pleased. She opened her mouth to say something, hesitated, and then closed it again.

'Mother, what was it you said you'd explain?' said Philip at once. 'We heard you say, "Yes, I'll explain". Was it something you had to tell us? What is it?'

'Don't say it's anything horrid,' said Lucy-Ann. 'Bill *is* coming away with us, isn't he?'

'Oh yes,' said Mrs Cunningham. 'Well – I hope you won't mind, my dears – but he badly wants us to take someone else with us.'

'Who?' asked everyone at once, and they all looked so fierce that Mrs Cunningham was quite surprised.

'Not his old aunt?' said Dinah. 'Oh, Mother, don't say it's someone we've got to be on our best behaviour with all the time.'

'No, of course not,' said her mother. 'It's a small boy – the nephew of a friend of Bill's.'

'Do we know him? What's his name?' asked Jack.

'Bill didn't tell me his name,' said Mrs Cunningham.

'Why can't he go to his own home for the holidays?' asked Dinah in disgust. 'I don't like small boys. Why should *we* have to have him? He'll probably spoil everything for us!'

'Oh no he won't,' said Philip, at once. 'Small boys have to toe the line with us, don't they, Jack? We get enough of them and their fatheadedness at school – *we* know how to deal with them all right.'

'Yes, but why has he got to come to *us*?' persisted Dinah. 'Hasn't he got a home?'

'Oh yes – but he's a foreigner,' said her mother. 'He's been sent to school in England to have a good English education. I should imagine his family want him to have a few weeks in a British family now, and experience a little of our homelife. Also, I gather there is some difficulty at his home at the moment – illness, I should think.'

'Oh well – we'll have to make the best of it,' said Lucy-Ann, picturing a very little, homesick boy, and thinking that she would comfort him and make a fuss of him.

'We'll park him with you then, Lucy-Ann,' said

Dinah, who didn't like small boys at all, or small girls either. 'You can wheel him about in a pram and put him to bed at night!'

'Don't be silly, Dinah. He won't be as small as that!' said her mother. 'Now – have you finished? It's almost lunchtime, so go and wash your hands and brush your hair.'

'Wash your hands, brush your hair, wipe your feet, blow your nose,' shouted Kiki. 'Brush your hands, blow your feet, wipe your – your – your . . .'

'Yes – you've got a bit muddled, old thing,' said Jack with a laugh. Kiki flew to his shoulder, and began to pull at Jack's ear lovingly. Then, as she heard the sound of the gong suddenly booming out, she gave a loud screech and flew into the dining room. She knew what *that* sound meant!

'Jack! Kiki will peck all the tomatoes if you don't keep an eye on her,' called Mrs Cunningham. 'Go after her, quickly!'

But there was no need to say that – everyone had rushed to the dining room at the first sound of the gong!

2

Arrival of Gustavus

The afternoon was spent in looking all over the house to see if any changes had been made, and in exploring the garden from end to end to see what flowers were out, what edible things there were (only lettuces, alas!) and to introduce Kiki to six new hens.

'There's a new carpet in the guest room,' said Lucy-Ann. 'But that's all the changes there are. I'm glad. I don't like to come home and find anything changed. I suppose this small boy will sleep in the guest room, Aunt Allie?'

'Yes,' said Mrs Cunningham. 'I'm getting it ready in a minute or two. Go and join the others in the garden. You can pick a few daffodils, if you like – we want some in the hall.'

Lucy-Ann wandered off happily. The very first day of the holidays was always heavenly. All the first few days went slowly, and the thought of days and days of holiday ahead was one to dwell on contentedly almost every minute.

'Lucy-Ann! Come here! Kiki's having the time of her life!' called Jack. 'Look at her showing off in front of the new hens!'

Kiki was sitting on a post in the hen run. The six hens were gathered admiringly around her.

'Cluck-cluck-cluck,' they said to one another, and one stretched herself on tiptoe and flapped her wings as if trying to fly. Kiki put her head on one side, stretched herself on tiptoe too, spread her wings wide and took off. She sailed down to the surprised hens.

'Cluck-luck-luck, urrrrrrk!' she said, earnestly. 'Cluck-luck-luck, urrrrrrk!'

'Cluck-uck-uck, cluck!' said the hens, in admiration, and went nearer. One hen daringly pecked at one of the parrot's tail feathers.

This was insolence! Kiki danced round the alarmed hens, making a noise like an aeroplane in trouble. The hens took to their heels and fled into the hen house, almost tumbling over one another as they tried to squeeze in at the narrow doorway two at a time.

Kiki waddled after them, clucking again. Mrs Cunningham called from a window.

'Children! The hens will *never* lay us eggs if you let Kiki scare them.'

'Kiki's gone into the hen house – she'll probably sit in a nesting box and try to lay an egg like the hens!' called Jack. 'Come out, Kiki.'

Kiki came back and looked inquiringly out of the little

doorway. 'Polly put the kettle on,' she said, peaceably, 'cluck-luck-luck, *urrrrrrk!*'

She flew to Jack's shoulder, and the hens looked at one another in relief. Was it safe to go out and wander round yet?

'There's the next-door cat,' said Dinah. 'Come to see what all the fuss is about, I expect! Hang on to Kiki, Jack.'

'Oh, she'll bark like a dog if the cat comes any nearer,' said Jack. 'Come on – let's see what the gardener has got in the greenhouse.'

It was a pleasant sunny afternoon, and the four really enjoyed themselves 'mooching about' as Jack called it. They all longed for Bill to arrive. Then the family would be complete – except, of course, that it would have one too many, if he really brought the unexpected boy with him!

'I'm going to watch at the gate for Bill,' announced Lucy-Ann after tea.

'We all will,' said Philip. 'Good old Bill! What luck for us that he's not on one of his hush-hush jobs just now, and can come away with us!'

They went to hang over the front gate together. Kiki kept putting her crest up and down excitedly. She knew quite well that Bill was coming.

'Bill! Pay the bill!' she kept saying. 'Where's Bill? Pop goes Bill!'

'You're a silly-billy,' said Lucy-Ann, stroking the parrot's soft neck. 'That's what you are!'

'*That's* an idiotic thing to call her,' said Dinah. 'Just as we're expecting Bill! She'll screech out "Silly-Billy" to him now, I bet you she will!'

'Silly-Billy, Billy-Silly!' shouted Kiki. She always loved words that sounded the same. Jack tapped her on the head.

'No, Kiki, stop it. Look, here's a car coming. Perhaps it's Bill's.'

But it wasn't. As it went by, Kiki hooted loudly – parp-parp-parp – exactly like a car.

The driver was astonished. He could see no car in sight. He sounded his horn, thinking there must be a hidden corner somewhere.

And then Lucy-Ann gave a squeal. '*Here's* Bill!' she said. 'A big black car, very sleek and shiny! Bill, Bill!'

She was right. It *was* Bill's car. It drew up at the front gate, and Bill's jolly face grinned at them as he looked out of the window. Somebody sat beside him. Was it the boy?

Bill opened the door and leapt out. The four children pounced on him. 'Bill! Good old Bill! How are you, Bill?'

'Silly-Billy!' screeched a voice.

'Ah – good evening, Kiki,' said Bill, as the parrot landed full on his shoulder. 'Still the same rude old bird. Aha! You want me at home to teach you a few manners!'

Kiki cackled like an excited hen. 'Now then – don't

you lay eggs down my neck!' said Bill. 'What are you cackling about? Where's your mother, Dinah?'

'There she is,' said Dinah, as Mrs Cunningham came running to the gate. Bill was about to call to her when an extremely loud cough came from the car – a cough that was meant to be noticed.

'Oh – I completely forgot for the moment,' said Bill. 'I've brought a visitor. Did you tell them, Allie?'

'Yes, I did,' said Mrs Cunningham. 'Where is he? Oh, in the car. Bring him out, Bill.'

'Come on out,' said Bill, and in the midst of a dead silence the owner of the loud cough slid out of the car in as dignified a manner as he could.

Everyone stared at him. He was about eleven, and certainly very foreign-looking. His blue-black hair was curly and rather longer than usual. His eyes were as black as his hair, and he had thicker lashes than either of the girls. And he certainly had magnificent manners.

He went to Mrs Cunningham, and took the hand she held out to him. But instead of shaking it he bowed over it and touched it with his lips. Mrs Cunningham couldn't help smiling. The four children stared in amusement.

'My thanks to you, dear lady,' he said, in a very foreign accent.

'That's all right,' said Mrs Cunningham. 'Have you had any tea?'

But before the boy chose to answer this question he had to make a further display of manners. He went to

13

Dinah, and before she knew what he meant to do, he took her hand and bent over it. She gave a squeal and snatched it away.

'Don't!' she said. Lucy-Ann put her hands firmly behind her back. She didn't want them kissed either. What an extraordinary boy!

'Gus, old fellow – we just shake hands, you know,' said Bill, trying to hide his amusement at the sight of the two girls' indignant faces. 'Er – this is Gustavus Barmilevo, Allie. He will be with us for the next few weeks, as his uncle has asked me to keep an eye on him.'

Gustavus Barmilevo bowed very low, but did not attempt any more hand-kissing. Bill introduced the rest.

'Dinah – Lucy-Ann – Jack – and Philip. I – er – hope you'll soon all be good friends.'

The two boys shook hands with Gus, eyeing him with much disfavour. Goodness! Were they to put up with this little foreigner all the holidays?

Gus did a funny little bow each time he shook hands. 'Plizzed to mit you,' he said. 'What is zis bird? How you call it?'

'It's a Kiki-bird,' said Jack, solemnly. 'Gus, meet Kiki. Kiki, meet Gus!'

Kiki held out her left foot as usual, to shake hands. Gus looked extremely surprised, but his manners remained perfect. He held out his hand to Kiki's foot. Unfortunately Kiki dug her talons into his fingers, and he gave a loud yell.

'What a noise, what a noise!' said Kiki, severely. 'Wipe your feet and blow your nose. Fetch the doctor!'

'My finger's blidding,' said the boy, with tears in his voice. 'It blids, look.'

'Fetch the doctor, Polly's got a cold, fetch the doctor,' chanted Kiki, enjoying herself. The boy suddenly realized that it was the parrot who was talking. He forgot his 'blidding' and stared at Kiki in amazement.

'It spiks!' he announced in awe. 'It spiks. It spiks words. It sees my blidding finger, and spiks to fetch the doctor. I never haf seen a Kiki-bird before.'

'Come along in, and I'll put a bit of bandage on your finger,' said Mrs Cunningham, getting tired of all this.

'Yes. It blids,' said Gus, mournfully, watching a minute drop of blood fall to the ground. He looked as if he was going to cry. Then he said a most extraordinary thing.

'This bird,' he said, looking at Kiki suddenly, 'the bird – it must be in a cage. I order it.'

'Don't be a fathead,' said Jack, after a moment's silence of astonishment. 'Come on, Aunt Allie – let's go indoors. Gus might "blid" to death!'

This was a most alarming thought, and Gus rushed into the house at once. The others followed slowly. What an extraordinary boy!

'Bit dippy,' said Dinah in a low voice, and they all nodded. Bill's voice hailed them.

'Hey! What about a spot of help with the luggage?'

'Oh, Bill. Sorry, we weren't thinking,' said Jack, and ran back at once. 'Gus rather took our breath away. What nationality is he?'

'Oh, he's a bit of a mixture, I think,' said Bill. 'Don't bother him about his family or his home, or he'll probably burst into tears. Sorry to inflict him on you like this. He'll be better when he's shaken down a bit. I believe he got on quite all right at the English school he was at. Anyway – I'll take him off your hands as much as I can, I promise you, as it's *my* friend who asked me to keep an eye on him!'

'We'll help, Bill,' said Lucy-Ann. 'I expect he's shy. Oh dear – I was so afraid he'd kiss my hand! What *would* the girls at school say?'

'Well, I should hardly think they'd know anything about it,' said Bill. 'You take that bag, Jack – and you that box, Philip. Well – it's nice to see you all home again! And Kiki, too, you old rascal. How *dare* you call me Silly-Billy?'

'Pop goes Billy, pop goes Billy!' screeched Kiki in delight, and flew down to his shoulder to nibble his ear. 'Pop-pop-pop!'

3

Gussy and Kiki

There really wasn't very much time that evening to get to know Gustavus Barmilevo. As they were all going off again the next day there was packing to do, and all kinds of arguments arose as to what was or was not to be taken.

Gustavus was bewildered by the noise of so many people talking at once. He sat staring at them all, nursing his bandaged finger. Kiki absolutely fascinated him. He watched her continually, but would not allow her near him.

As soon as she came near, he flapped his hands at her as if she was a hen. 'Go off!' he cried. 'Clear away!'

'He's as muddled as Kiki sometimes gets,' said Jack, with a grin. 'Kiki can't make him out. Now, where did I put that book? Aunt Allie, did I pack that big book?'

'You did,' said Aunt Allie. 'And I have unpacked it. For the third time, Jack, you are NOT going to take a score of books about birds. Two is more than enough, so make your choice.'

'You're so hardhearted,' groaned Jack. 'Well, I suppose you will allow me to take my field glasses? In fact, if they don't go, I shan't go either.'

'You can carry those round your neck,' said Mrs Cunningham. 'Do try and remember that there will be seven of us in the car and all the luggage, too. We really must take the least luggage possible. Kiki, bring that string back. KIKI! Jack, if you don't stop Kiki running off with absolutely everything I put down for a moment, I shall go mad.'

'Where is the cage?' suddenly demanded Gustavus, in a commanding voice. 'Put him in the cage.'

'She's a her, not a him,' said Jack, 'and stop talking about cages. No ordering about, please!'

Gustavus apparently did not follow this, but he resented Jack's firm voice. He sat up stiffly.

'This bird iss – iss – wicket!' he said. 'Not good. Wicket. I will not haf him wizzout a cage.'

'Now, Jack, now!' said Mrs Cunningham warningly, as she saw Jack's furious face. 'He's not used to Kiki yet. Or to our ways. Give him a chance to settle down. Don't take any notice of him. Gustavus, the bird is not wicked. She is good. Sit still and be quiet.'

'Where is the cage?' repeated Gustavus, in a most maddening manner. 'A beeg, BEEG cage. For a wicket bird.'

Jack went over to him and spoke slowly and loudly with his face close to the surprised boy's.

'I have a beeg, BEEG cage,' he said, most dramatically. 'But I keep it for small, annoying boys. I will bring it for you, Gus. If you want a beeg, BEEG cage you shall have it for yourself. You shall sit in it and be safe from that wicket, wicket bird.'

To Jack's enormous surprise Gustavus burst into tears! All four children looked at him aghast. How *could* a boy of eleven be so incredibly upset? Even Lucy-Ann was shocked. Mrs Cunningham hurried over to him.

'He's tired out,' she said to the others. 'It's all strange to him here, and he's never seen a parrot like Kiki before. Nor have any of us, come to that! Cheer up, Gustavus. Jack didn't mean what he said, of course.'

'I jolly well did,' began Jack. 'Kiki's old cage is enormous and . . .'

Mrs Cunningham firmly led the weeping Gus from the room. The others stared at one another in complete disgust.

'Well! To think we've got to put up with *that* these hols!' began Jack. 'All I can say is that I'm going to take him firmly in hand – and he won't enjoy it one bit!'

'I'll take him in hand, too,' said Dinah, quite fiercely. 'Who does he think he is – laying down the law about Kiki and a cage! Oh, Jack – I do wish you'd got that old cage and brought it in. I'd have loved to see Gustavus's face.'

19

'Poor old Gussy!' said Lucy-Ann. 'Wouldn't he have howled! Poor Gussy!'

'Gussy!' said Kiki, at once. 'Fussy-Gussy! Fussy-Gussy!'

Everyone laughed. 'You've hit it off again,' said Philip to Kiki. 'Fussy – that's exactly what we'll have to put up with – fuss and grumbles and silliness all the time. Why didn't his parents bring up their kid properly? Fussy-Gussy! We shall get jolly tired of him.'

'Fussy-Gussy!' screamed Kiki, dancing to and fro, to and fro on her big feet. 'Wipe your feet, Gussy!'

'Dry your eye, you mean,' said Philip. 'I hope Gussy's not going to burst into tears *too* often. I think I'll borrow one of Mother's afternoon teacloths and take it with me to offer him every time he looks like bursting into tears.'

Mrs Cunningham came back, and overheard this. 'I think you're being a bit unkind,' she said. 'He may seem a bit of a nuisance, I admit – but it must be rather nerve-racking for him to be plunged into the midst of a company like this when he doesn't speak the language properly, and everyone laughs at him. I think you should play fair and give him a chance.'

'All right, Mother,' said Philip. 'All the same – it isn't like Bill to thrust someone like Gussy on us at a moment's notice, just at the beginning of the hols.'

'Well, you see,' said his mother, 'it's like this. Bill was saddled with this youngster – and he knew you wouldn't like having him. So he suggested to me that he should go off with him alone somewhere. I couldn't bear that, because a holiday without Bill would be horrid – and so we thought it would be best if Gustavus came with us all, and we tried to put up with him. It's either that or going without both Gussy *and* Bill.'

'I see,' said Philip. 'Well, I'd rather put up with Gussy than have no Bill.'

'That's what *I* thought,' said his mother. 'So don't make Bill feel too bad about it, will you? He's quite likely to vanish with Gussy for the rest of the holidays if you make too much fuss. All the same – I think you can quite safely help young Gustavus to join in. That won't do him any harm at all. He seems frightened and shy to me.'

'We'll soon show him exactly where he stands,' said Jack. 'But I really can't think how Bill was soft enough to take him on. Where's Gustavus now?'

'I've popped him into bed with a book,' said Mrs Cunningham. 'There's such a lot of things to do this evening and I really felt I couldn't cope with upsets and bickerings the very first day you were home – so I thought everyone would be happier if he was in bed.'

'How right you were!' said Jack. 'Well, now dear Gussy is safely out of the way, let's get on with things. I suppose you don't want any help with the supper, Aunt Allie?'

'I imagine that's a roundabout way of saying you are

hungry again?' said Aunt Allie. 'All right – the girls can see to supper. You boys come and help me finish packing the greatest number of things into the smallest possible bags! I'm leaving behind practically everything belonging to Gustavus – he's got the most *ridiculous* things – pyjamas made of real silk, for instance! And monograms on everything.'

'He must have gone through an awful lot of teasing at school then,' said Philip. 'I'm surprised they didn't have his hair cut. Most *girls* would envy him all that long curly hair. Couldn't we get his hair cut, Mother?'

'Possibly,' said his mother. 'Let's not talk about him any more.'

The packing was finished by supper time. Mrs Cunningham was determined not to take more than a change of clothes for everyone: shirts, jerseys, blazers and macs. Once more she had to take Jack's enormous book on birds from where he had hidden it yet again under some shirts in a suitcase. She looked at him in exasperation.

He grinned back amiably. 'Oh, sorry, Aunt Allie! You don't mean to say it's got itself packed again!'

'I'm *locking* the cases now,' said Aunt Allie, with determination. 'Really, Jack, I sometimes feel you want a good spanking!'

Supper was a hilarious meal. Gustavus, having a tray of food in bed, listened rather enviously. He was tired, and glad to be in bed – but it did sound very jolly downstairs. He didn't somehow feel that he had made a very good impression, though. That bird – it was that 'wicket' bird who had made things go wrong. When he got Kiki alone he would slap her hard – biff!

Gustavus brought his hand down smartly as he pictured himself slapping Kiki. The tray jerked and his lemonade spilt over the traycloth. There – that was thinking of Kiki again. He was so engrossed in trying to mop up the mess he had made that he didn't notice someone rather small sidling in at the door.

It was the parrot, come to find out where Gustavus was. Kiki's sharp eyes had missed him at supper time. Then where was he? Upstairs?

Kiki went under the bed and explored the slippers and boxes there. She pecked at one of the boxes, trying to get off the lid. She loved taking off lids.

Gustavus heard the noise. What was it? He looked round the room.

Peck-peck-peck! The lid wouldn't come off. 'Who's there? Who iss it?' said Gustavus, in an anxious voice.

Kiki debated what noise to make. She had a grand store of noises of all kinds. There was the screech of a railway train going through a tunnel. No – that would bring Mrs Cunningham upstairs, and she would be angry. There was the lawn mower – a most successful noise, but also not very popular indoors.

And there was quite a variety of coughs – little short

hacking coughs – deep hollow ones – and sneezes. What about a sneeze?

Kiki gave one of her most realistic sneezes. 'A – WOOOOOSH-OO!' It sounded very peculiar indeed, coming from under the bed.

Gussy was petrified. A sneeze – and such an enormous one – and under the bed! WHO was under the bed? Someone lying in wait for him? He began to tremble, and the lemonade spilt again.

Kiki began to cough – a deep, hollow cough, mournful and slow. Gustavus moaned. Who was it *coughing* under his bed now? He didn't dare to get out and see. He was sure that whoever was there would catch hold of his ankles as soon as his feet appeared on the floor.

Kiki next did a very fine growl, and poor Gussy shivered so much in fright that his tray nearly slid off the bed altogether. He just clutched it in time. But a plate fell off, hit one of his shoes standing nearby and rolled slowly under the bed.

Now it was Kiki's turn to be surprised. She hopped out of the way and glared at the plate, which flattened itself and lay still.

'Help! Help!' suddenly yelled Gussy, finding his voice at last. 'Someone's under my bed. Help! Help!'

Bill was up in a trice, striding over to Gustavus. 'What is it? Quick, tell me.'

'Under the bed,' said Gussy, weakly, and Bill bent down to look. There was nobody there. Kiki had decided that the joke was over, and was now safely inside the nearby wardrobe, her head on one side, listening.

'You mustn't imagine things, old chap,' Bill was saying kindly. 'There's nobody under the bed – and never was. Nobody at all! I'll take your tray and you can settle down to sleep!'

4

Off to Little Brockleton

Next day was bright and sunny, with big piled up clouds racing over the April sky.

'Like puffs of cotton wool,' said Dinah. 'I hope it's going to be like this all the hols.'

'I'm going to get the car,' said Bill. 'When I hoot I shall expect you all to be ready. Allie, you can sit in front with me, and Lucy-Ann must squeeze there too, somehow. The other four can go at the back. Luggage in the boot. And if anyone wants to be dumped on the road and left to walk, he or she has only got to behave badly, and I'll dump them with pleasure.'

'I really believe you would too, Bill,' said Lucy-Ann.

'Oh, not a doubt of it,' said Bill, putting on such a grim face that poor Gussy was really alarmed. He made up his mind that he would behave superlatively well, and he immediately put on his finest manners. He opened doors for everyone. He bowed. He tried to take whatever Mrs Cunningham was carrying, and carry it for her.

When he got into anyone's way, which he did almost every minute, he sprang aside, bowed, and said:

'Excuse, plizz. I pollygize.'

'Polly put the kettle on,' said Kiki, at once. 'Polly, Polly-Polly-gize.' Then she went off into an alarming cackle of laughter.

'How's your finger, Gus?' asked Jack, politely.

'It has stopped blidding,' said Gus.

'Well, I warn you – don't try and play tricks with old Kiki,' said Jack, 'or she'll go for you – make you blid again – much, much blid!'

'Ah, wicket,' said Gus. 'I think that bird is not nice.'

'I bet Kiki thinks the same of you!' said Jack. 'You're standing in my way. You'd better move unless you want this suitcase biffing you in the middle.'

'Excuse, plizz. I pollygize,' said Gussy, hurriedly, and skipped out of the way.

At last everything was ready. Mrs Cunningham's cleaner came to see them off, promising to lock up after them, and come in every day to clean and dust. Bill was hooting loudly. Gussy was so terribly afraid of being left behind that he shot down the front path at top speed.

Bill, Mrs Cunningham and Lucy-Ann squeezed them-selves into the long front seat. The other four got into the back. Gussy shrank back when he saw that Kiki was going with them, apparently on Jack's shoulder, next to him.

Kiki made a noise like a cork being pulled out of a bottle – POP! Gussy jumped.

Kiki cackled, and then popped another cork. 'POP! Pop goes the weasel. Gussy. Fussy-Gussy, Gussy-Fussy. POP!'

'What do you think you're doing, Gussy?' said Jack, seeing the boy slipping from the seat down to the floor.

'Excuse, plizz. I pollygize. The Kiki-bird, he spits in my ear – he goes POP!' explained Gussy, from his seat on the floor.

Everyone roared. 'Don't be an ass, Gussy,' said Jack. 'Come on up to the seat. Squeeze in at the other end if you like, next to Dinah. But I warn you – Kiki will wander all over the car when she's tired of sitting on my shoulder.'

'Blow your nose,' said Kiki sternly, looking down at the surprised Gussy.

'All ready, behind?' called Bill, putting in the clutch. He pressed down the accelerator, the engine roared a little and the car moved off down the road.

'Heavy load we've got,' said Bill. 'What a family! This car is going to grunt and groan up every hill!'

It did, though it was a powerful car, and one that Bill used in his work. It swallowed up the miles easily, and Mrs Cunningham was pleased to think they would arrive at their destination before dark.

'What is the name of the place we are going to, Aunt

Allie?' asked Lucy-Ann. 'Oh yes, I remember – Little Brockleton. Are we having a cottage, or what?'

'Yes,' said Aunt Allie. 'It's called Quarry Cottage, because an old quarry is nearby. It's about a mile from the village, and I believe only a farmhouse is near. We can get eggs and butter and milk and bread from there, which is lucky.'

'I shall ask about badgers as soon as I get there,' said Philip, from the back. 'I wish I could get a young badger. I've heard they make wonderful pets.'

'There! I knew you'd start hunting out pets of some kind,' said Dinah. 'We never can have a holiday without your bringing in mice or birds or insects or even worse creatures.'

'I've been thinking of studying *spiders* these hols,' said Philip, seriously. 'Amazing creatures, spiders. Those great big ones, with hairy legs, are . . .'

Dinah shivered at once. 'Let's change the subject,' she said. 'I don't know why, but whenever anyone even *mentions* spiders I seem to feel one crawling down my back.'

'Oh, gosh – don't say my spider's escaped!' said Philip at once, and pretended to look through his pockets. Gussy watched him in alarm. He didn't like spiders either.

Dinah gave a small shriek. 'Don't be mean, Philip – please, please. You haven't *really* got a big spider, have you?'

'Philip!' called his mother warningly. 'You'll be dumped in the road. Remember what Bill said.'

'All right. I haven't got a spider,' said Philip, regretfully. 'You can sit in safety, Di. I say, Gus, aren't you uncomfortable down there, on the floor, among our feet? I keep forgetting you're there. I hope I haven't wiped my feet on you yet.'

'That is not a nice thing to spik,' said Gussy, with dignity. 'I will be angry to have your feets wiped on me.'

'Let's play a game,' said Jack, seeing an argument developing. 'We'll look out for black dogs – white cats – piebald horses – red bicycles – and ice cream vans. The one who is last to reach a hundred must stop at the next ice cream van and buy ices for us all!'

This sounded exciting to Gussy. He scrambled up from the floor at once, and squeezed himself beside Dinah. Bill and Mrs Cunningham heaved a sigh of relief. Now there would be quite a bit of peace – everyone would be looking out and counting hard.

Gussy was not at all good at this game. He missed any amount of black dogs and white cats, and kept counting ordinary horses instead of piebald ones. He looked very miserable when he was told that he couldn't put all the brown and white horses he had seen into his score.

'He's going to cry!' said Philip. 'Wait, Gus, wait. Take my hanky.'

And he pulled out one of the kitchen tablecloths, which he had neatly purloined just before coming away, in spite of his mother's threats.

Gussy found the tablecloth pushed into his hands. He looked at in astonishment – and then he began to laugh!

'Ha ha! Ho ho! This is cloth, not hanky! I will not weep in this. I will laugh!'

'Good for you, Gussy!' said Jack, giving him a pat on the back. 'Laugh away. We like that!'

It was quite a surprise to everyone to find that Gussy could actually laugh at a joke against himself. They began to think he might not be so bad after all. He stopped playing the counting game after that, but displayed even more surprising behaviour at the end of the game.

Lucy-Ann was last to reach a hundred. She felt in her little purse for her money, knowing that she must buy ice creams for everyone, because she had lost the game.

'Please, Bill, will you stop at the next ice cream van?' she said. So Bill obligingly stopped.

But before Lucy-Ann could get out, Gussy had opened the door at the back, shot out and raced to the ice cream van. 'Seven, plizz,' he said.

'Wait! *I* lost, not you!' shouted Lucy-Ann, half indignant. Then she stared. Gussy had taken a wallet out of his pocket – a wallet, not a purse! And from it he took a wad of notes – good gracious, however many had he got? He peeled off the top one and gave it to the ice cream man, who was as surprised as anyone else.

'You come into a fortune, mate?' asked the ice cream man. 'Or is your dad a millionaire?'

Gussy didn't understand. He took his change and put

it into his pocket. Then he carried the ice creams back to the car, and handed round one each, beaming all over his face.

'Thanks, Gus,' said Bill, accepting his. 'But look here, old chap – you can't carry all that money about with you, you know.'

'I can,' said Gussy. 'All the term I had it here in my pocket. It is my pocket money, I think. They said I could have pocket money.'

'Hm, yes. But a hundred pounds or so in notes is hardly *pocket* money,' began Bill. 'Yes, yes – I know you kept it in your *pocket*, but real pocket money is – is – oh, you explain, boys.'

It proved to be very difficult to explain that all those pound notes were not pocket money merely because Gussy kept them *in* his pocket. 'You ought to have handed them in at your school,' said Philip.

'They said I could have pocket money,' said Gussy, obstinately. 'My uncle gave it to me. It is mine.'

'Your people must be jolly rich,' said Jack. 'I bet even Bill doesn't wander round with as many notes as that. Is Gus a millionaire or something, Bill?'

'Well – his people *are* well off,' said Bill. He slipped in the clutch again and the car slid off. 'All the same, he'll have to hand over those notes to me. He'll be robbed sooner or later.'

'He's going to cry,' reported Dinah. 'Philip, quick – where's that tablecloth?'

'I am not going to weep,' said Gussy, with dignity. 'I am going to be sick. Always I am sick in a car. I was yesterday. Plizz, Mr Cunningham, may I be sick?'

'Good gracious!' said Bill, stopping very suddenly indeed. 'Get out of the car, then, quick! Push him out, Dinah. Why, oh, why did I let him have that ice cream? He told me yesterday he was always carsick.'

Mrs Cunningham got out to comfort poor Gussy, who was now green in the face. 'He *would* be carsick!' said Dinah. 'Just the kind of thing he'd have – carsickness.'

'He can't help it,' said Lucy-Ann. 'Anyway, it's all over now. He looks fine.'

'Plizz, I am better,' announced Gussy, climbing back in the car.

'Keep the cloth,' said Philip, pushing it at him. 'It might come in useful if you feel ill again.'

'Everyone ready?' called Bill. 'Well, off we go again. We'll stop for lunch at one o'clock, and then we'll be at Little Brockleton by tea time, I hope. Gussy, yell if you feel queer again.'

'I am only sick once,' said Gussy. 'Plizz, I have lost my ice cream. Will you stop for another?'

'I will not,' said Bill, firmly. 'You're not having any more ice creams in the car. Doesn't anyone want a nap? It would be so nice for me to drive in peace and quietness! Well, next stop, lunch!'

5

Quarry Cottage

Little Brockleton was a dear little village. The car ran through it, scattering hens and a line of quacking ducks. Bill stopped at a little post office.

'Must just send off a message,' he said. 'Won't be a minute. Then we'll go and call at the farmhouse to ask the way to Quarry Cottage, and to pick up eggs and things, and order milk.'

He reappeared again after a moment. The children knew that Bill had to report where he was each day, because urgent jobs might come his way at any moment – secret tasks that only he could do.

They went off to the farmhouse. The farmer's wife was delighted to see them. 'Now, you come away in,' she said. 'I've been expecting you this last half-hour, and I've got tea for you. You won't find anything ready at the cottage, I know, and a good tea will help you along.'

'That's very kind of you,' said Mrs Cunningham, gratefully. 'My goodness – what a spread!'

It certainly was. It wasn't an ordinary afternoon tea, it was a high tea. A fresh ham, glistening pink. A veal and ham pie smothered in green parsley, like the ham. Yellow butter in glass dishes. A blue jug of thick yellow cream. Honey. Home-made strawberry jam. Hot scones. A large fruitcake as black as a plum pudding inside. Egg sandwiches. Tea, cocoa and creamy milk.

'I'm absolutely determined to live on a farm when I'm grown up,' said Jack, looking approvingly at all the food on the big round table. 'I never saw such food as farm houses have. I say, isn't this smashing?'

Gussy felt glad that Mrs Cunningham had insisted that he should eat very little at lunch time. He felt sure he had an appetite three times bigger than anyone else's.

'What will you have?' asked the farmer's wife, kindly, seeing his hungry look.

'I will have some – some pig meat,' said Gussy. 'And some pie meat with it. And I will have some cream with it, and . . .'

'He's a little comedian isn't he?' said the farmer's wife, with a laugh. 'Pig meat! Does he mean ham? And surely he'll be sick if I pour cream over it all?'

'Cut him a little ham, if you will,' said Mrs Cunningham. 'No pie. He can't possibly eat both. And of course not the cream!'

'I have ordered my meal,' said Gustavus, in a very haughty voice, staring at the surprised farmer's wife. 'I will have what I say. Plizz,' he added as an afterthought.

35

'Shut up, Gus,' said Bill. 'You'll do as you're told. You're forgetting yourself.'

'I have not forgot myself,' said Gus, puzzled. 'I have remembered myself, and I want . . .'

'Shut up,' said Bill, and Gus shut up.

The others grinned. It was nice to see Bill squashing Gussy. Gussy was very angry. He glared at Bill, and seemed about to say something. But Bill looked across at him, and he didn't say it. Bill winked at the others, and they winked back.

'Fussy-Gussy,' remarked Kiki, from Jack's left shoulder. 'Ding-dong-bell, Gussy's in the well.'

'Pussy's in the well, not Gussy,' corrected Jack. 'Oh, you pest – you've nabbed a strawberry out of the jam!'

The farmer's wife took Kiki in her stride, and was not unduly surprised at her, nor annoyed. 'My old aunt had a parrot once,' she said. 'One like yours here. She didn't talk as well as yours though.'

'Is she alive?' asked Jack, thinking that it would be fun to put the two parrots together and see them eyeing one another. What kind of conversation would they have?

'Is who alive? My aunt or her parrot?' asked the famer's wife, pouring out cups of creamy milk. 'The parrot's dead. It was supposed to be over a hundred years old when it died. My old aunt is still alive, though. There she is, sitting by the fire over in the corner. She's my great-aunt really, and *she'll* be more than a hundred if she lives another ten years.'

The five children stared in awe at the old woman in the corner. She looked rather like a witch to them, but her eyes were faded blue, instead of green. She smiled a dim smile at them, and then bent her white head to her knitting again.

'She's a real worry sometimes,' said the farmer's wife. 'She wanders round and falls about, you know. And the doctor's off on a week's holiday soon, and what I shall do if old Aunt Naomi falls and hurts herself then, I don't know! There's no neighbours near but you – and you're a good bit away!'

'You send a message to us if you want us at any time,' said Mrs Cunningham at once. 'I'll certainly come. I am quite good at first-aid and nursing. So don't worry about the doctor going. Send a message if you want us.'

'Ah, yes – I could do that,' said the farmer's wife. 'Thank you kindly. Now – who wants a bit of that fruit-cake? It's good, though I shouldn't say it, seeing that I made it myself.'

'If I eat any more I shan't be able to move a step,' said Bill, at last. 'Will you kindly make up your minds to finish, you kids? We'll get along to Quarry Cottage, and settle in. Did you manage to send someone in to clean up the place for us, Mrs Ellis?'

'Oh yes,' said the farmer's wife. 'And she took eggs, milk, a pie, some home-made cheese, ham and butter and new bread for you. Oh yes, and a side of bacon. You won't do too badly down there! Come along to me when you want anything. I hope you have a good, restful holiday.'

They left the cosy farmhouse reluctantly. Jack eyed Gussy suspiciously, as the got into the car. 'You look a bit green,' he said. 'Sure you'll be all right in the car?'

'He'll be all right,' said Mrs Cunningham, hurriedly. 'It's not very far – he'll be *quite* all right.'

'Wishful thinking, Aunt Allie!' said Jack. 'Kiki's very quiet. Kiki, *you've* made a pig of yourself too – a little pig, eating such a big tea!'

Kiki gave a big hiccup. Nobody ever knew if her hiccups were real or put on. Mrs Cunningham always felt quite certain that they were put on.

'Kiki!' said Jack, severely. 'Manners, manners!'

'Pardon,' said Kiki. Gussy stared at her in amazement. It was surprising enough for a parrot to hiccup, but even more surprising that she should apologize! He quite forgot to feel sick because of his astonishment at Kiki.

Down a winding lane – up a little hill – down another lane whose hedges were so high that the children felt they were in a green tunnel. Round a sharp bend, and then there was Quarry Cottage, standing a little way back from the lane.

It was a pretty place, its garden full of primroses, wallflowers and daffodils. The people who owned it had gone to the South of France for a holiday, and had been pleased to let it to Bill.

The windows were rather small, as they always are in

old cottages. The door was stout, made of oak darkened by the years, and was protected by a small porch, thatched with straw like the sloping roof of the cottage.

'A thatched cottage – how lovely!' said Lucy-Ann. 'I don't know why, but thatched houses always look as if they belong to fairy-tales, not to real life. It's a dear little place.'

They went up the path. Bill had the key and unlocked the door. In they all went, exclaiming over everything.

'I need hardly remind you that this house, and every-thing in it, belongs to someone else,' said Mrs Cunningham. 'So that we'll have to be extra careful – but as you will probably be out of doors most of the day you won't have time to do *much* damage!'

'We shouldn't anyway,' said Jack. 'Not with Bill here ready to jump on us!'

The cottage was just as pretty inside as out, and very cosy and comfortable. The three boys had a big attic, the two girls had a small bedroom over the sitting room, and Bill and his wife had a larger one next to it.

The larder was full of food! Mrs Ellis, the farmer's wife, had certainly remembered them generously. Mrs Cunningham heaved a sigh of relief as she looked at the ham and bacon, eggs and milk. Housekeeping was not going to be the nightmare she had expected!

'You two girls unpack everything,' she said. 'We've not brought much with us, so it won't take you long. Arrange the boys' things in the big chest in their room – there's enough room for the clothes of all three there.'

'I cannot slip with others,' announced Gustavus, coming down the stairs into the hall, where the girls and Mrs Cunningham were undoing the suitcases. 'Never have I slipt with others.'

'What are you talking about?' said Dinah. 'Nobody wants you to slip. Why should you?'

'He means *sleep*,' said Lucy-Ann. 'Don't you, Gussy?'

'It is what I said,' said Gussy. 'I may not slip with others. At school I slipt by myself. Here I will slip by myself also. It iss the rule of my family.'

'Well, it isn't the rule here,' said Dinah. 'Get off those shirts, Gus. And don't be an ass. There are only three bedrooms, anyway.'

'What's the argument?' said Bill, coming in after putting the car into a shed, and seeing Gussy's frowning face.

'It's Gus,' said Dinah, piling her arms full of clothes. 'He's just announced he wants to sleep by himself. Says it's the rule of his family. Who does he think he is? A prince?'

Gussy opened his mouth to reply, and Bill hurriedly interrupted what he was going to say. 'Gus, you'll sleep with the two boys here. Understand?'

'I slip alone,' said Gus, obstinately. 'Never have I . . .'

'There's a tiny little box-room he could have,' said Dinah, suddenly, a gleam in her eye. 'I saw it just now, when I was upstairs. He could "slip" there. I'm sure he won't mind the dozens of colossal spiders there – ugh, they've all got hairy legs. And I heard a mouse – or it might have been a rat – scuttling behind the cistern – and . . .'

Gus looked horrified. 'No. I do not slip with spiders and mouses,' he said. 'But still it is not right that I should slip with Philip and Jack. And I will not slip with that wicket bird.'

'Come in here a minute, Gus,' said Bill, and he took the boy firmly by the shoulder, led him into the sitting room and shut the door. The two girls heard a murmur of voices, and looked at one another in surprise.

'Mother, what's all the fuss about?' said Dinah, puzzled. 'Why doesn't Bill put that silly young Gus in his place? If he's going to be high and mighty all the time, and give his orders, and act in such an idiotic way, we're all going to hate him.'

'Leave it to Bill,' said her mother, and then changed the subject. 'Take those things up, Dinah – and Lucy-Ann, put these things in my room, will you? Now, did I pack Bill's set of pipes, or didn't I?'

The girls went upstairs. 'Mother's as mysterious about Gus as Bill is,' said Dinah, crossly. 'Is there some mystery about him? Can he be a Prince in disguise, or something?'

'What! A funny little boy like him!' said Lucy-Ann, in disgust. 'Of COURSE not!'

6

Mostly about Gussy

It was fun settling in at Quarry Cottage. Mrs Cunningham was pleased and happy. She hadn't been looking forward to a holiday for seven people, five of them children, knowing that she would have to do everything for them, and that perhaps the shopping would be difficult.

But it was easy. The village was not too far away, even for walking purposes. The farmhouse was willing to supply a wonderful selection of good food. Mrs Gump, the tiny little charwoman, came every day, and was cheerful and hardworking. She also liked children, which was a great blessing.

She didn't like Gussy, though. 'He orders me about, that one,' she complained. 'He even wanted me to go upstairs and fetch his handkerchief for him, Mam. He's staying with you, isn't he? Well, I'm not going to be ordered about by anyone, specially not little nippers like that.'

Gussy was very difficult those first days. He didn't like this and he didn't like that. He complained if he was given a cracked plate. He absolutely refused to make his bed, though it was a rule in the house that everyone should make their own.

'I do not make beds,' he announced, in his haughtiest manner. 'Mrs Gump shall make my bed.'

'Mrs Gump shall not,' said Dinah, firmly. 'You go and make your own – and for goodness' sake don't make such a *fuss*, Gussy.'

'Fussy-Gussy, Fussy-Gussy!' chanted Kiki, in delight. 'Fussy-Gussy, Fussy . . .'

Gus caught up a book and flung it at Kiki. The bird dodged easily, sat on the back of a chair and cackled with laughter. Gus was just about to pick up another book when he found himself on his back on the floor.

Dinah had put up with enough from Gussy. She had now lost her temper, and was showing him how well she could do it! She banged his head on the floor, and he yelled the place down.

Mrs Cunningham came in at once. 'Dinah! What are you thinking of? Get up at once. Go upstairs and stay there till I come to you.'

'He flung a book at Kiki,' panted Dinah, rising up red and angry. Gussy still lay on the floor, and the tears ran down his cheeks.

'Get up, Gussy,' said Mrs Cunningham. 'I'm just as

cross with you as I am with Dinah. Go up to your room too, and stay there.'

'You cannot order me,' said Gussy, with as much dignity as he could manage through his tears. 'Send this girl back home. And that wicket bird.'

'GO TO YOUR ROOM!' said Mrs Cunningham in such a furious voice that Gussy leapt to his feet, tore up the stairs, went into his room, slammed the door and turned the key!

Bill came in. 'It's Gussy again,' said his wife. 'He's such a little *fathead*. I hope this is going to work out all right, Bill. I think we should have thought of some other idea. The others don't understand, you see. Can't we tell them?'

'I'll have a word with Gussy again,' said Bill. 'If he doesn't come to heel I'll take him away by myself – but I thought it would be so much safer if he was here with all of us.'

He went upstairs. Mrs Cunningham also went up to Dinah. Lucy-Ann was with her, arranging the clothes in the drawers. Dinah was very mutinous.

'It's all very well,' she said, when her mother scolded her, 'but why should Gussy spoil everything for us? He's always interfering, always ordering us about, always wanting the best of everything for himself – and fancy DARING to try and hurt Kiki!'

'I understand how you all feel,' said her mother. 'So does Bill. But he's promised to keep an eye on Gussy for the next few weeks, and he must. I think perhaps it would be best if he took Gussy off somewhere, and left us here by ourselves.'

'Oh, *no*,' said Lucy-Ann at once. 'No, Aunt Allie! You've married him, and he belongs to us now. Please don't let him do that! Dinah, *say* something!'

'Well – I thought, I *could* put up with Gussy, rather than have Bill leave us,' said Dinah. 'But – but – oh dear, I *can't* promise not to go for Gussy. I don't think I'll be able to stop myself! And I can't possibly let Bill go away either.'

'Well, stay here by yourself for an hour and make up your mind,' said her mother, losing patience. 'Lucy-Ann, come downstairs with me.'

Nobody told Jack or Philip about Gussy flinging a book at Kiki. Kiki didn't forget though! She plagued the life out of poor Gussy! He never knew when she was under the table ready to tweak his toes at the end of his sandals. He never knew when she would hide in his bedroom and wait for him to come up. Then she would produce one of her extraordinary noises and send him downstairs in a panic at top speed!

'Well, if Bill didn't punish him – and I don't think he did – *Kiki's* doing it all right!' said Dinah to Lucy-Ann. 'Anyway, Gussy is certainly better. I wish he wasn't coming on the picnic with us today, though.'

A picnic had been arranged for everyone on Sugar-Loaf Hill. It was really the name that had attracted the children – Sugar-Loaf Hill! What a lovely name!

They set off together, Bill and the boys carrying the food in satchels on their backs. Gus had made a fuss, of course. He seemed to think that it was a great indignity to carry something on his back.

'Never haf I done this before,' he protested. 'In my country it is the – how do you call it? – donkeys who carry for us. Why do you not haf donkeys? I will not be a donkey.'

He was puzzled at the shouts of laughter that greeted this speech. 'Oh, Gus – you'll be the death of me,' said Jack. 'Do you mean to say you didn't *know* you were a donkey?'

'It is bad to call me thát,' said Gussy, frowning. 'In my country you would . . .'

'Oh, gee-up, donkey, and stop fussing,' said Philip, giving Gussy a shove. 'Leave your satchel behind, if you like. No one will mind. It's got your lunch in, but nobody else's! We're carrying the girls' lunch, and Bill's got Mother's. You've only got your own.'

'So chuck it into the bushes, then you won't have to carry it like a donkey,' said Dinah, with a squeal of laughter. 'Go on, Gus!'

But Gus didn't. He thought better of it, and took the satchel of food on his back, though he looked extremely annoyed about it.

Sugar-Loaf Hill was just like its name – it was very like a sugar-loaf, cone shaped but flat at the top, and was covered with primroses, cowslips and dog-violets.

'We ought to be able to see quite a good way from the top,' said Jack, as they toiled up. It was a stiff pull up but at last they were at the top. A strong breeze blew round them, but the sun was hot, so it was very pleasant to feel the wind blowing by.

'I say! Gussy carried his lunch after all!' said Jack, pretending to be surprised. 'My word, I'm hungry.'

They all were. They ate every single thing they had brought, and Kiki had a good share, too, especially of the bananas. She loved holding a banana in one foot and biting big pieces off it.

Gussy sneezed. Kiki immediately sneezed too, a much bigger sneeze than Gussy's. Then Gussy sniffed, a little habit he had which annoyed Mrs Cunningham very much.

Kiki sniffed too. 'Stop it, Kiki,' said Mrs Cunningham. 'One sniffer is quite enough.'

'Polly's got a cold,' said Kiki, and sniffed again, exactly like Gussy. Gussy took no notice but after a minute he suddenly sniffed again.

'Blow your nose!' shouted Kiki. 'Where's your hanky! Gussy's got a cold, send for . . .'

'Be quiet, Kiki,' said Jack. 'Gussy, don't keep sniffing. If you do, you'll set Kiki off and she'll do nothing but sniff too.'

'I do not sniff,' said Gussy. 'That bird is wicket and too clever. It should have a cage.'

'Shut up, Gus,' said Bill, who was now leaning back, enjoying a pipe. 'Remember what I said to you.'

Gus apparently remembered. He subsided and lay back and closed his eyes. The others sat and looked at the view. It was marvellous, for they could see a great way off.

'That's the village over there,' said Philip, pointing. 'And there's the farmhouse. And you can just see the tops of the chimneys and a bit of one end of the thatched roof belonging to Quarry Cottage. In those trees, look.'

'And there's the road we came by – the main road,' said Jack. 'Where are my field glasses? Would you pass them, Di. Gosh, I can see miles with these. I can see the way the main road twists and turns; I can see the traffic on it – looking just as small as the toy cars we used to have, Philip. Have a look.'

Philip put the glasses to his eyes. They really were magnificent ones. He could see for miles, just as Jack had said. 'Yes – it's queer to see the cars and the lorries looking like toys, going along those ribbony roads,' said Philip. 'Now – there's a black car – rather like Bill's. I'm going to watch it and see how far I can follow it.'

The others lay back, half asleep, listening to Philip's voice. The sun was hot now, and they didn't feel inclined to go walking after such a big picnuc,

'Yes – it's on the main road still,' said Philip, staring through the glasses. 'There it goes – a good speed too. Jolly good speed. May be a police car, perhaps.'

'You can't tell a police car so far away,' said Jack. Bill

looked up from his newspaper. He knew a lot about police cars!

'Tell me its number and I'll tell you if it's a police car,' he said. The boys laughed.

'That's clever of you, Bill,' said Jack, 'but you know jolly well you're safe – you can't possibly read the number at this distance. Still got the car, Philip?'

'Lost it for a bit,' said Philip. 'It's gone behind some buildings – no, there it is again. It's come to crossroads – it's gone across. Now it's stopped.'

Gussy gave a little snore which Kiki immediately copied. Philip went on with his car story.

'A man got out – I think he must have gone back to look at the sign post. He's got into the car again. Yes, they missed their way, they're backing. Ah, I thought so – they've turned down the other road – the road that leads to our village.'

'You'll tell us it's at Quarry Cottage next,' said Jack, sleepily. 'You're making all this up now, *I* bet!'

'I've lost it again. No, here it comes,' said Philip, pleased. 'Yes, it's going through the village – down into the lane. It's stopped again. I think they're asking the way from someone – a labourer probably. Can't see from here. On they go again – and they've turned up the farm road! They're going to the farmhouse. Probably rich relations of Mrs Ellis.'

Bill put down his paper abruptly and reached out for the glasses. He focused them on the farmhouse and saw the car immediately – a big one, obviously expensive. He studied it intently for a minute and then handed back the glasses without a word.

'Do you know the car, Bill?' asked Jack, curiously, seeing Bill's expression.

'No,' said Bill. 'I don't. But – it just makes me think a bit, that's all. Sorry I can't tell you any more. I'll wander up to the farmhouse tonight and ask a few questions – then I'll know a bit more!'

7

A surprising announcement

Philip and Jack were more interested in the car, after Bill's remarks. They took it in turns to keep an eye on it, but it simply stayed where it was for twenty minutes, and then went away, taking the same route as it came.

'It's gone, Bill,' said Philip. 'I expect it was only some visitor. I say, look at Gussy! His mouth is wide open. Let's put something into it.'

'Let sleeping donkeys lie!' said Jack. 'And don't put ideas into Kiki's head! She'll hunt around for something now to pop into Gussy's mouth.'

Philip looked round at everyone. Only Bill and Jack were awake besides himself. He put his hand into his pocket and brought out something – something small and brown and pretty. It sat up on his hand.

'I say! You've got a dormouse! What a pet! said Jack. 'Don't let Dinah see it – she'll have a fit.'

'I got it on the way here,' said Philip. 'I saw it sitting on a branch and it let me pick it up.'

'It would!' said Jack, enviously. 'You've got some magic about you, Philip. I've never seen an animal yet that didn't come under your spell. Isn't he a pretty little fellow?'

'I've called him Snoozy,' said Philip, stroking the tiny creature, whose large black eyes shone like mirrors in his head. 'Dormice are very dozy, snoozy things. I must remember to buy some nuts from the grocer's next time we go to the village. Snoozy will like those. We won't tell Dinah. He'll live comfortably in my pocket. I've had dormice before – they're very tame.'

'How nice to keep putting your hand in your pocket and feeling a furry dormouse there!' said Jack. 'Hallo – do I hear voices?'

The boys looked in the direction of the voices. They saw two men, obviously farm labourers, taking a path near the foot of the hill, talking together.

'I think I'll just scoot down and ask them if they know anything about badgers here,' said Philip. 'Coming, Jack?'

The two boys ran down the hill. The men heard them coming and looked round. 'Good afternoon,' panted Philip. 'Do you mind if I ask you a question or two? It's about badgers.'

'Badgers – what may they be?' said the younger man.

'Eee, man – you know badgers,' said the older man. 'Brocks, they be.'

'Oh, the brocks,' said the younger fellow. 'No, I don't know nothing about *them*. Never seed one in my life.'

'That's a-cause you sleeps in your bed every night!' said the other man, with a laugh. 'Brock, he comes out at night. I sees him many a time.'

'You're an old poacher, you are, Jeb,' said the younger man. 'Out at nights when honest folk are asleep. That's how you see the brocks!'

'Maybe, maybe,' said the older man, with a twinkle in his bright eyes. He turned to the boys. 'What are you wanting to know about the brocks?' he said.

'Well – I'd like to watch them,' said Philip at once. 'I'm keen on wild creatures – all kinds. I've not had much chance of seeing badgers, though. Where can I see them around here? We're at Quarry Cottage.'

'Ah, so that's where you be,' said the old man. 'Then you'll find old Brock not far away from you, little master. You may see him in the woods on the east side of the cottage – that's the most likely place – or you may see him down in the old quarry. I saw a badger's sett there – his den, you know – last year. I knew he had his hole down there by the big pile of earth he'd taken out of it.'

'Yes – that's right. He always does that,' said Philip, wishing he could get to know this old fellow. He felt sure that he would be able to tell him many tales. 'Well, thanks very much. We'll watch in both places.'

'There's owls in the quarry too,' said the old man. 'Little owls, and barn owls and tawnies. They go there for the rats and mice. I've heard them – the barn owls – screeching their heads off. Frighten the life out of you, they do!'

'I know,' said Jack, making up his mind at once that he would go and watch in the quarry. He liked owls very much. Perhaps he could get a young one and tame it. But he'd have to be careful not to let it see Snoozy the dormouse. That would be the end of Snoozy!

The boys walked off together, exploring the cone-shaped hill. A shout from above attracted their attention.

'Jack! Philip! We're going back in a minute. Are you coming with us, or do you want to follow sometime later?'

'We'll come now,' shouted Jack, and he and Philip began to climb up towards the others. They found Gussy awake but scowling. He spat something out of his mouth as they came up.

'Manners, manners!' said Jack, reprovingly.

'He says somebody popped bits of grass into his mouth,' said Dinah, with a giggle. 'So he keeps on spitting them out. Did *you* put them in, Jack?'

'No,' said Jack. 'And Philip didn't either.'

'There you are!' said Dinah, triumphantly, turning to the angry Gussy. '*Nobody* put anything in your mouth when you were asleep. You're just making it all up. I bet you chewed a bit of grass yourself.'

'I did not,' said Gussy. 'It was a wicket thing to do. It nearly chocked me. I was chocked.'

'Choked, you mean,' said Lucy-Ann. 'Well, it's a mystery. Nobody did it – and yet you were nearly "chocked" with grass. Don't spit any more. You *can't* have any left in your mouth now.'

Jack and Philip threw a quick look at one another. They knew quite well who had played this trick on poor Gussy. Gussy saw the look and rounded on them. 'You know who did it! I saw you look!'

'All right. We know who did it,' said Jack. 'A jolly good trick too. We thought of doing it ourselves, you looked so silly with your mouth wide open, snoring.'

'I do not snore,' said Gussy. 'And tell me who did it.'

'Come on,' said Bill. 'I expect it was old Kiki. She's done it before – to me! Can't you see a joke, Gus?'

Gus suddenly exploded into his own language. He stood there, shaking his long hair back, his face scarlet, and a string of incomprehensible words coming from his mouth. Nobody understood a thing.

Kiki was intensely interested with this string of words she didn't understand. She sat herself on Jack's shoulder, near to the angry Gus, and listened intently. When he stopped for breath, she continued on her own.

'Gibberollydockeryblowykettlefussy-gussy,' she began, and poured out strings of nonsense into which she wove many of the words she knew, mixed up with ones she didn't! Everyone roared. It sounded exactly as if Kiki was talking to Gus in his own language.

Gus was silenced. He stared at Kiki, amazed. 'Does

she spik English now?' he demanded. 'What does she spik?'

'She's spikking a lot of nonsense, bad bird!' said Jack. 'Be quiet, Kiki. Don't show off!'

Bill and Mrs Cunningham had already set off down the hill. The girls followed, giggling. Gus was annoying but he really did provide them with a lot of amusement.

Gus followed them at last, shaking back his long hair defiantly. He spat now and again as if he still had grass in his mouth, and Kiki copied him with joy, going off into cackles of laughter every now and again.

It was about half-past five when they got back to Quarry Cottage. 'If any of you want tea after that enormous lunch, will you please get yourself a glass of milk, and some biscuits?' said Mrs Cunningham. 'Or a bit of fruit cake if you feel real pangs of hunger?'

All the five children apparently felt real pangs, for they raided the larder and reduced the fruitcake to a mere fragment of itself. They also drank all the milk, much to Mrs Cunningham's dismay.

'Now we've none for your cocoa tonight or for breakfast tomorrow!' she said.

'I'll get some at the farm when I slip up this evening,' said Bill. 'It will be a good excuse to go up and ask a few questions.'

'Any mystery on?' enquired Dinah. 'I'm never sure about you, Bill! Even in the middle of a holiday I always wonder if you've got a hush-hush job on as well.'

'Mystery or not, Bill always keeps his eyes open!' said Philip. 'It's part of your job, isn't it, Bill?'

'Let's play a game,' said Dinah. 'Where are the cards? Let's play Racing Demon. Do you play it, Gus?'

'I play it,' said Gus. 'I played it at school last term. I am good with this game. Very good. I go as fast as this.'

He pretended to be putting cards down, and was so vigorous that his hair fell over his eyes. He pushed it back. He was always doing that, and it got on Dinah's nerves.

'Your long hair!' she said. 'It's always in the way.'

'Now don't start anything,' said Jack. 'A spark is enough to set him off. Talk about being touchy! Don't glare like that, Gus, you make me shake at the knees!'

'Poof!' said Gus, rudely.

'Poof!' said Kiki at once. 'Poof, poof, poof!'

'That'll do,' said Jack. 'One poofer is quite enough in the family. Got the cards, Di? Oh, good!'

They were soon sitting in a ring on the floor, playing Racing Demon. Kiki couldn't understand the game at all and wandered off into a corner because Jack wouldn't let her pick up any of the cards.

'Poof!' they heard her say to herself quietly. 'Poof!'

Surprisingly enough Gussy *was* good at Racing Demon. He was very deft with his cards, and very sharp to see which pile he could put them on. He got very excited, and panted loudly. His hair fell over his eyes, and he pushed it back. Jack calmly put a card on a pile that

Gus was just about to put one on, and Gus exclaimed in annoyance.

'I was going to put mine there – but my hair fell over me!'

'Why do you *have* hair like that then?' said Dinah. 'It's really very long. Why don't you get it cut?'

'Yes, that's a good idea,' said Philip, putting a card down. 'We'll go into the village tomorrow and see if there's a barber. He'll cut it shorter for you, Gus. You'll get a crick in your neck, tossing your hair about like that!'

'Yes. Good idea! We'll have it cut tomorrow,' said Jack, grinning at Gus.

Gus surprised them. He flung down his cards, stood up, and went scarlet in the face. 'Short hair is for boys like *you*,' he said, scornfully. 'It is not for me. Never must I have my hair short. In my country always it is the custom for such boys as me to wear their hair long!'

'Such boys as you!' echoed Jack. 'What do you mean? You've got a very high opinion of yourself, my lad. You may come from a rich family, but you act like royalty, and it won't do. You're not a Prince, so don't try and act like one. It only makes you ridiculous.'

Gus drew himself up to his last inch. He threw back his hair once more. 'I *am* a Prince!' he said, dramatically. 'I am the Prince Aloysius Gramondie Racemolie Torquinel of Tauri-Hessia!'

8

Bill explains

There was a dead silence after this dramatic announcement. Nobody said a word, not even Kiki. They all stared in astonishment at Gus, not knowing whether to believe a word of what he had said.

Then his lips began to shake, and he tried to press them together firmly. Lucy-Ann was sure he wanted to cry again!

'I have broke my word!' suddenly wailed Gus. 'I am a Prince and I have broke my word!'

A voice came from behind them. It was Bill's.

'Yes, you have broken your word, Aloysius Gramondie Racemolie Torquinel. And your uncle told me you would *never* do that. How am I to keep you safe if you break your word?'

Bill came forward, his face stern. Everyone stared at him in alarm. Whatever was up?

'Bill – he's not *really* a Prince, is he?' said Jack.

'Believe it or not, he is,' said Bill. 'His uncle is the King of Tauri-Hessia.'

'Well! That explains his peculiar behaviour,' said Dinah. 'His ordering people about – and his high and mighty airs – and all his money and boasting.'

'And his long hair too,' said Bill. 'The Princes in his country never have their hair cut short as ours do. They wear it a certain length, as you see. It's bad luck on him, really, because he gets teased. Still, the boys at his school knew who he was and knew he couldn't help it, and he didn't have too bad a time.'

There was a pause while the four took a look at Prince Aloysius. He shook back his hair and Dinah groaned.

'I wish you wouldn't do that, Gussy. I can't call you Ally – Ally-something or other. You'll have to go on being Gussy.'

'Oh, he must,' said Bill, at once. 'I gave him the name of Gustavus Barmilevo for a special reason. Things – rather serious things – are happening in his country at the moment, and it's essential that he should go under another name here.'

'What serious things are happening?' said Jack. 'Revolts or something?'

'Well, I'll tell you,' said Bill. 'His uncle is King, and as he has no children, Gussy is the heir to the throne. Now there are certain people in Tauri-Hessia who don't like his uncle or the firm way in which he governs the country.

Incidentally he governs it very well, and our own Government thinks him a very sound ruler.'

'I can guess what's coming,' said Jack. 'Those who don't like the strong uncle think it would be a good thing to get a weak youngster, who'll have to do what they tell him, and put *him* on the throne. Then they can do as they like!'

'Exactly,' said Bill. 'And so they are on the look-out for Gussy here. If they can get hold of him and put *him* on the throne, he will have to do exactly what he's told. His uncle will be imprisoned or killed.'

'And Gussy knows all this, does he?' asked Philip.

'He knows all right!' said Bill. 'Everything was explained to him. He's fond of his uncle; he doesn't want to be used as a kind of pawn by his uncle's enemies – and so he was put in my keeping, and told to be merely a foreign schoolboy called Gustavus. And here he is.'

'I have broke my word to you,' said Gussy, sounding very doleful. 'Mr Bill, I ask you to pardon me.'

'Well, don't do it again, that's all,' said Bill. 'Nobody here is likely to give you away, fortunately – we are all your friends – or would like to be if only you'd behave yourself a bit better.'

'I behave better at once immediately,' said Gussy, emphatically.

'Hm. Well, we'll see,' said Bill, drily. 'It would help considerably if you could try to behave like the others so that if any stranger comes hanging round he'll think you are an ordinary schoolboy staying with friends. At present I think you're behaving rather stupidly, not like a Prince at all. In fact, if I were a Tauri-Hessian citizen, I'd be sorry to think I'd have *you* as King when you grew up.'

'Bill – is it the Tauri-Hessian Government or ours that has asked you to have charge of Gussy?' said Dinah.

'Both,' said Bill. 'It's important to both Governments that there should be a sound, strong ruler in Tauri-Hessia. I can't tell you why at present. I think it's possible that all this will blow over in a few weeks, and then Gussy can go back to school in safety. In the meantime, we've got to make the best of all this.'

'Yes. I see everything now,' said Dinah. 'You should have told us at first. Bill. We'd have understood better.'

'I had orders not to say a word except to your mother,' said Bill. 'She had to be in on this, of course. I took this cottage because it was well hidden and nobody would guess that Gussy would be here. And I thought if you all came too, he would be even better hidden – hidden in the midst of you, one of many, so to speak.'

'You're clever, Bill,' said Lucy-Ann, slipping her hand in his. 'We'll look after Gussy. We won't let him out of our sight. Gussy, we're your friends.'

'I thank you,' said Gussy, with a funny little bow. 'It is an honour.'

'That's the way to talk,' said Bill, and gave him a clap on the back. 'Now then, everyone – you've got to forget all about Aloysius Gramondie and Tauri-Hessia. Got that?'

'Yes, Bill,' said everyone. They looked rather solemn. It was peculiar to have serious and unusual problems suddenly presented to them candidly in the middle of a game of Racing Demon. The ordinary and the extraordinary didn't really mix. They turned with relief to their game again, as Bill went out of the room to find his wife and tell her what had happened.

'*Look* what Kiki's been doing while we've been talking!' said Jack, in exasperation. 'Mixing up all the cards. Put down the ones you're holding, Kiki!'

'She's been playing a quiet little game by herself,' said Lucy-Ann, with a laugh. 'And she's holding two cards in her foot eactly as if she was waiting for her turn to go. Put them down, Kiki.'

'One, two, three, six, eight, four, one,' said Kiki, getting her numbers muddled up as usual. 'Three, four, buckle my shoe.'

'One, *two*, buckle my shoe,' said Lucy-Ann. 'Your memory's going, Kiki!'

Kiki gave a hiccup, as she often did when she thought she had made a mistake.

'Enough, Kiki,' said Jack. 'Anyone want another game?'

Nobody really felt like one after all the revelations Bill had made. They didn't like to discuss them in front of Gussy, though they were longing to talk about them.

Mrs Cunningham put her head in at the door. 'Bill's going up to the farm for milk. Anyone want to go with him? Not Gussy, he says.'

'I'll go,' said Lucy-Ann, scrambling up. 'I'd like a walk. You boys stay with Aunt Allie, and look after her.'

'Right,' said Jack, thinking it was just as well to do so, with prospective kidnappers and revolutionaries about, even although they might be as far away as Tauri-Hessia.

'I'll stay behind too,' said Dinah. 'I've got a blister on my foot.'

So Lucy-Ann went off happily with Bill. She liked getting him alone. He was always jolly and full of fun when they were all together, but Lucy-Ann thought he was even nicer alone. She slipped her hand through his arm, and they walked off in the dusk together.

'In case you want to say anything about Gussy, I'll just warn you not to,' said Bill, in a low voice. 'I don't want the slightest suspicions to get about that he's not all he seems. It would be a very serious thing for him if he were forced to be King at his age.'

'I won't say anything,' said Lucy-Ann in a whisper. 'Let's talk about Jack.'

'You're always ready to talk about Jack, aren't you?' said Bill, amused. 'Well, I must say that Jack has got something I'd dearly like to have myself.'

'What's that? Kiki?' asked Lucy-Ann.

'No – a very nice little sister,' said Bill. 'It's good to see a brother and sister so fond of one another.'

'Well, our mother and father died when we were very young,' said Lucy-Ann, 'so we only had each other. But now we've got you and Aunt Allie, and we've got Philip and Dinah as well. We're lucky!'

'I'm lucky too,' said Bill. 'A nice ready-made family for me! Hark at the owls hooting round. What a collection of hoots!'

'That was the little owl,' said Lucy-Ann, who had been well trained in bird calls by Jack. 'That "tvit-tvit-tvit" noise. And that lovely long quavering hoot is the tawny owl.'

'And what in the world is *that*?' said Bill, suddenly startled by a loud screech near his head. Lucy-Ann laughed.

'The screech owl – the old barn owl!' she said. 'He does that to frighten the mice and the rats.'

'Well, he scared me too,' said Bill. 'Ah – is that the farmhouse looming up? It is. You come in with me, Lucy-Ann, and don't be surprised at my conversation with Mrs Ellis!'

They knocked at the door and went into the big, cosy kitchen. Although it was a warm night there was a fire in the chimney corner, and old Aunt Naomi sat there, knitting, huddled up in a shawl.

Mrs Ellis hurried to meet them. 'Well, it's good to see you! And how are you getting on? Settled in nicely? That's right. Now, what can I do for you? Sit you down, do!'

They sat down. Lucy-Ann found a rocking chair and began to rock to and fro. A big tabby came and jumped into her lap, settled down and went to sleep. Lucy-Ann felt quite honoured.

Mrs Ellis brought her a piece of cake, and she nibbled at it and listened lazily to Bill. He gave Mrs Ellis all the news first. Then he went on to talk about Quarry Cottage.

'It's a lovely, peaceful spot,' he said. 'I shouldn't think strangers ever come along here, do they, Mrs Ellis? Except people like ourselves who want to stay for a bit.'

'Now, it's funny you should say that,' said Mrs Ellis, 'because two strangers came to our farmhouse this very afternoon – in a lovely black car. Rather like yours, Mr Cunningham.'

'I suppose they lost their way,' said Bill. Although he spoke in his ordinary voice Lucy-Ann knew that he had pricked up his ears at once.

'No, they hadn't lost their way,' said Mrs Ellis. 'They'd been hunting round for a nice farmhouse to stay in for a few days – the man's wife has been ill, and simply longed to be in a quiet farmhouse, with good food. Somebody told him of our farm, and they came to enquire.'

'I see,' said Bill. 'And – er – did you say you would take them, Mrs Ellis?'

'I did,' said Mrs Ellis, 'though my husband scolded me for it. He says my kind heart runs away with me! They're coming tomorrow. They said their name was Jones – but it's my belief they're foreigners!'

'Foreigners,' said Bill, slowly. 'Yes – I had an idea you were going to say that!'

9

An afternoon out

Lucy-Ann stopped rocking the chair, and her heart sank into her shoes. Foreigners! Did that mean they were from Tauri-Hessia, or whatever the country was – and had they tracked down Gussy? Oh dear – surely, surely another adventure wasn't beginning! This had seemed as if it would be such a nice peaceful holiday.

'Blow!' whispered Lucy-Ann to the cat on her knee. 'Blow Gussy! Blow his uncle!'

Bill asked a few more cautious questions, but Mrs Ellis had nothing else to tell him of any interest. He got up, took the milk she had brought him from the dairy, and paid her. He thanked her, said good night, and out he and Lucy-Ann went, into the starry night.

'I fear – I very much fear – that somebody is on Gussy's track,' said Bill, in a half-whisper as they went along together. 'Now, how could they have guessed he was with us? It's a pity he's so striking-looking, and so easily recognizable. I suppose someone must have spotted him with me, made enquiries about me – and as soon as they knew who I was, the rest would be easy. Hm! I don't like it very much.'

'Will you and Gussy have to disappear from here?' whispered Lucy-Ann, so softly that Bill could hardly hear. 'Please don't go away, Bill.'

'I'll have to discuss things with your aunt,' said Bill. 'Don't say a word to Gussy. He'll get the wind up properly, if I know anything about him. And on no account must any of you leave him alone anywhere – always keep him in your midst.'

'Yes, Bill,' said Lucy-Ann. 'Oh dear – I do wish those people weren't going to the farm. Bill, they *might* be ordinary people, mightn't they? They haven't *got* to be enemies, have they?'

Bill squeezed Lucy-Ann's hand. 'No. I may be wrong. But I get hunches about these things, Lucy-Ann. And I've got a hunch this very minute. You needn't worry. I shan't let anything happen.'

'Well – so long as you're with us,' said Lucy-Ann. 'But please don't go away, Bill.'

'I won't,' said Bill. 'Not unless I take Gussy with me, which would really be the safest thing to do.'

They reached Quarry Cottage, and went in. Gussy and Dinah had gone to bed. Aunt Allie and the boys were still up, reading.

Bill put the milk in the larder and came back. He sat

down and told the three of them what Mrs Ellis had said. Mrs Cunningham looked grave.

'How did they know he was down here?' she wondered. 'Oh, Bill – what shall we do now? Shall we leave here at once – all of us?'

'No. That would tell the enemy too much,' said Bill. 'I don't see that two people – a man and a woman – can do very much by themselves – I mean they can't fall on us and wrest Gussy away from our midst! As long as there are only the two of them we haven't much to fear – and Mrs Ellis will soon tell us if any more arrive. One of the boys can go up each day for milk, and get the latest news.'

'Right. We'll go on as we are then,' said his wife, and Lucy-Ann heaved a sigh of relief. 'You'll tell Gussy of course, Bill – put him on his guard? He's got to be very sensible now – keep with us all, not wander away – and I'm afraid the boys must fasten their window at night.'

'Blow!' said Jack, who hated a shut window at night. 'Kiki's enough of a sentinel, Aunt Allie. She would screech the place down if anyone came.'

'I'd feel safer with your window shut,' said his aunt. 'I think Kiki *would* screech. Still – I don't want to run any risks.'

Gussy was told the next morning, and so was Dinah. Philip was posted up by the farm to watch the new people arrive. They came in the same black car that Philip had seen through his field glasses the day before. It was long and low and large – and very expensive-looking.

'A Daimler,' said Philip. 'I bet that can get along! Now – can I spot what the visitors are like?'

There were two. One was a spruce, tall, lean man, wearing a very well cut suit, an eyeglass in one eye, and hair smoothly brushed back. The other was a woman – pretty, young and with a very foreign voice. The man spoke English well, but he was obviously a foreigner too.

He handed the woman out very carefully indeed. Then she leaned on his arm as they walked up the path to the farmhouse door. They went very slowly.

'Either she's been ill or she's pretending to be,' thought Philip. 'I'd better go back and tell Bill – and Gussy too. He may recognize them from my description.'

But Gussy didn't. He shook his head. 'No, I don't know them.'

'I wouldn't be surprised if they come along here some-time today,' said Bill. 'Just to have a snoop round. I feel sure they know I'm at this cottage – and that Gussy may be with you all on holiday!'

Bill was right. That afternoon, while Jack was bird-watching near the house, he heard the sound of voices. He peeped through the bushes. It must be the visitors from the farm! The man had an eyeglass in his eye, as Philip had described – and the woman was walking slowly, leaning on his arm.

Jack sped indoors by the back way. 'Bill! he called. 'They're coming. Where's Gussy? He could peep at them as they go by and see if he knows them!'

Gussy ran to a front window and hid behind the curtain, waiting. But the couple from the farm didn't go by! They turned in at the front gate and came right up to the cottage door. A sharp sound came on the afternoon air.

Rat-a-tatta-TAT!

Mrs Cunningham jumped. She was having a rest on her bed. Bill opened the door and went in.

'Allie! It's the couple from the farm. What nerve to come right to the house! They obviously don't think that we suspect anything at all. Will you go down and open the door? I shan't appear – and Gussy mustn't either. The others can, of course.'

Bill went to tell Gussy to keep out of the way and Mrs Cunningham ran down the stairs to the front door, patting her hair tidy. She opened it.

Two people stood on the step, a man and a woman. The man raised his hat politely.

'Forgive this sudden visit,' he said, 'but my wife and I were taking a short walk, and she has begun to feel faint. A cup of water would help her, I think – if you would be so kind?'

'Oh – do come in,' said Mrs Cunningham, hoping that Gussy wouldn't come running down the stairs. 'I'll get some water.'

She took them into the little sitting-room. The woman sank down into a chair and closed her eyes.

'My wife has been ill,' said the man. 'I have brought her down to the farm for a few days – good air, and good food, you know – better than any hotel! But I should not have taken her so far on her first day.'

'I'm so sorry,' said Mrs Cunningham, playing her part as best she could. 'Dinah! Where are you? Get a jug of water and a glass, will you, dear?'

Dinah sped to the kitchen, and came back with a glass jug of ice-cold water, and a glass on a little tray. She put them down on the table and looked curiously at the couple. They looked back at her.

'And is this your daughter?' said the woman. 'What a nice child! Have you any other children?'

'Oh yes,' said Mrs Cunningham. 'Another of my own and two adopted ones. Fetch them, Dinah.'

Dinah went to fetch the others. They came in politely, Lucy-Ann, Philip and Jack. The woman screamed when she saw Kiki on Jack's shoulder.

'A parrot! Don't let it come near me, I beg of you!'

'Wipe your feet,' ordered Kiki. 'Shut the door. Grrrrrrrrr!'

The woman gave an exclamation in a foreign language, and said something to the man. He laughed.

'My wife says that people who come to visit you should have good manners, or your parrot will soon teach them,' he said. 'So these are your four children. But have you not a fifth?'

'No,' said Mrs Cunningham. 'Only these four belong to me.'

'I thought Mrs Ellis said there was another little boy,' said the woman, sipping the water.

Mrs Cunningham reached for the jug and refilled the woman's glass, hoping that she would not pursue the subject of the 'other little boy'. But the woman persisted.

'Perhaps you have a little boy *staying* with you?' she said, sweetly, smiling at Mrs Cunningham.

'Oh, I expect Mrs Ellis means Gussy,' said Mrs Cunningham. 'Little Gussy is staying for a while – till his family can take him home.'

'And may we not see the little Gussy?' said the woman. 'I love children. Do not leave this little Gussy out.'

'Anyone know where he is?' said Mrs Cunningham, in a voice that made the four children quite certain that she didn't want them to know. They didn't know, anyway! Gussy was at that moment in the wardrobe upstairs, where he had put himself straight away at the first sound of the knock on the door. Bill had thought he might as well stay there!

'I've no idea where Gus is,' said Jack. 'Doing something on his own, I expect. Do *you* know where he is, Philip?'

'No idea,' said Philip. 'Messing about somewhere, probably out in the woods.'

'Ah – he likes to wander about, does he?' said the man. 'Well – we may see him when we go back to the farm. Thank you, Madam, for being so kind to my wife. May I please give your four nice children something to buy ice creams with? And here is something for the little missing Gussy also.'

To the children's surprise he put down a five-pound note on the table in front of Mrs Cunningham. She pushed it back at once, quite horrified.

'Oh no – please! I couldn't hear of it. We only got you a glass of water. No, no – take this back. I couldn't possibly allow the children to have it.'

The man looked surprised and rather uncomfortable. He put the note back in his pocket. 'Just as you please,' he said. 'In *my* country it is only a courtesy to return a kindness.'

'What is your country, sir?' asked Jack, at once. 'Aha!' he thought. '*Now* we'll bring you out into the open.'

The man hesitated, and the woman gave him a quick glance. 'My country – oh, I come from Italy,' he said. 'A beautiful land. Come, my dear, we must go.'

He took his wife's arm and led her to the door, his eyes searching everywhere for the missing Gussy. He bowed to Mrs Cunningham and went down the path.

She called a sentence after him, and he turned. 'What do you say?' he said. 'I didn't understand.'

Mrs Cunningham repeated it. He looked puzzled,

bowed again, and went out of the gate. He disappeared with his wife up the lane.

'Well, *he's* not from Italy!' said Mrs Cunningham. 'I called out to him in Italian to say that he was to give my best wishes to Mrs Ellis – and he didn't understand a *word*!'

10

An urgent call

Jack slipped out to make sure that the couple went back to the farm. He came back to report that they had and Bill held a conference at once. Gussy had been hauled with difficulty out of the wardrobe.

He had recognized the woman but not the man. 'She is Madame Tatiosa,' he said. 'The wife of the Prime Minister. I hate her! She is clever and sharp and cruel.'

'What – that pretty young woman?!' said Mrs Cunningham in astonishment.

'Yes,' said Gussy, nodding his head vigorously. 'Once she was a spy for our country. My uncle told me. A very clever spy. And she married the Prime Minister, and tells him what to do.'

'Hm,' said Bill. 'And you didn't know the man, Gussy? Not that that matters. You've recognized one of them and so we know for certain that they're after you. I almost think we'd better clear out. I really don't know what to do for the best! I think I'd better take you and hand you over to the keepers in the Tower of London! You'd at least be safe there!'

'But you said, Bill, that if there were only two of them, the man and the woman, they couldn't very well do anything to Gussy,' said Jack. 'Why not let one of us keep watch each day to make sure no other car comes down to the farm – or no other visitor? I can easily go and spend the day at the farm, and watch – and Philip can watch the next day.'

'I think perhaps you're right,' said Bill, puffing at his pipe. 'Anyway – we'll stay put for the next two days, and wait for the enemy to make the next move. There's no doubt that they think Gussy's the boy they want. I expect Mrs Ellis has described him carefully to them – and he's easily described!'

'Yes – long hair, for one thing,' grinned Jack. 'Shall I nip along to the farm now, Bill, and keep watch for the rest of the day? I can go and ask for some butter or something, and then hang round, helping with a few jobs. I'd like that, anyway.'

'Right. You go,' said Bill, and Jack sped off with Kiki on his shoulder. The others got up to go for a walk, well away from the farm! 'Take your tea,' said Mrs Cunningham. 'Nobody will know where you are, if you go off for a walk, so nobody will be able to find you! You should be quite safe, Gussy!'

So Gussy, Philip and the two girls went off with a picnic basket. They walked for about two miles and then found a glade that was golden with polished celandines. They sat down, hot with their walk.

'This is heavenly,' said Lucy-Ann. 'I do love celandines. They look as if someone polished them every single morning. Jolly good workman he must be – he never misses a petal!'

Dinah gave a scream. 'Oh – what's that on your shoulder, Philip! Oh, it's a mouse!'

Philip's dormouse had decided that the pocket he lived in was getting too hot for his liking. So he had squeezed his way out, run up Philip's vest, and appeared through the opening of his collar. There he was now, sitting up on the boy's shoulder.

'Oh – a *dor*mouse!' cried Lucy-Ann in delight. 'What's his name, Philip? Will he let me hold him?'

'His name is Snoozy and it suits him,' said Philip. He felt in a pocket and brought out a nut. He gave it to Lucy-Ann. 'Here, take this, offer it to him on the palm of your hand and he'll run over to you.'

Lucy-Ann balanced the nut on her palm and held it out to the tiny mouse, being careful not to move too quickly. The dormouse watched her hand coming close to Philip's shoulder, and his whiskers quivered as his nose twitched.

'He can smell the nut,' said Philip. 'Keep quite still, Lucy-Ann. There he goes! How do you like the feel of his tiny feet?'

'Oh, lovely!' said Lucy-Ann. 'Isn't he a *dear*, Philip. I wish I had one too.'

'I'll try and get you one,' said Philip.

But Dinah gave a squeal at once. 'No! She sleeps with me, and I'm not having mice in the bedroom.'

'But this is a *dor*mouse, not a housemouse,' said Lucy-Ann. 'It doesn't smell, or anything. It's just perfectly sweet.'

Snoozy nibbled daintily at the nut. A bit broke off and he took it into his front paws, sitting up just like a squirrel. He looked at Lucy-Ann out of his bright eyes.

'He's got such big black eyes that they really are like mirrors,' she said. 'I can see my own face, very tiny, in each of them.'

'*Can* you?' said Gussy, in surprise and put his face close to Lucy-Ann's to look into the big eyes of the dormouse. It fled at once, disappearing down Philip's neck at top speed.

'You moved too fast, Gussy,' said Lucy-Ann crossly. 'You *would* manage to startle him.'

'Excuse, pliss. I pollygize,' said Gussy. 'I beg your pardon, Lucy-Ann.'

'All right. But I do hope Snoozy will come back,' said Lucy-Ann, rather cross.

He peered out of Philip's neck once or twice, but he wouldn't come right out. 'He's not *absolutely* tame yet,' explained Philip. 'I've not had him long enough. But he soon will be. He'll be coming out at meal times soon and nibbling his little nut on my bread-plate.'

'Not if I can help it,' said Dinah.

'Don't be silly,' said Philip. 'You simply don't *try* to like dormice. You . . .'

'Someone coming,' said Lucy-Ann, suddenly. Her sharp ears had caught the sound of voices.

'Get under the bush, Gussy,' ordered Philip. 'Go on, quick!'

Gussy vanished at once, and the bush closed over him. It was a pity it was a gorse bush, but Gussy didn't have time to think of prickles.

Two men came by, talking in the broad accent of the countryside. One was the man who had told Philip so much about badgers. He waved to him.

'It'll be a good night for badgers tonight!' he called. 'Moonlight – and that's what they like.'

'Come out, Gus,' said Philip, when the men had passed. 'False alarm.'

Gussy crawled out, scratched on face, hands and knees by the gorse prickles. He was very frightened.

'He blids,' said Dinah unkindly. 'Gus, you are blidding all over.'

'It's nothing much,' said Philip, taking out his handkerchief and scrubbing the drops of blood away here and there. 'Everyone gets pricked by gorse sooner or later. Cheer up, Gus. And for goodness' sake don't complain.'

'I don't like blidding,' said poor Gussy, in a woebegone voice. 'It makes me feel sick.'

'Well, be sick then,' said hard-hearted Dinah. 'But don't make a FUSS.'

Gussy made a valiant effort and swallowed hard. He didn't fuss after all. What a victory!

After they had eaten every crumb of their tea, they decided to go back. Philip wanted to have a look at the quarry on the way to see if he thought that badgers might really make that their haunt.

He wandered round the big deserted place, examining the hedges round for signs of a badger's sett. The girls and Gussy ran the few hundred yards that lay between the quarry and the cottage. Lucy-Ann thought they ought to, in case any enemy was lying in wait!

'Any news?' she asked, as they went indoors, panting. 'Has Jack come back from the farm yet?'

He hadn't. Nobody had any news at all, it seemed. Jack had none either, when he came.

'Not a soul came to the farm,' he said. 'And I didn't even see the man and the woman. They must have been in their room all the time. Once I heard a "ting" – as if somebody was using the telephone. It might have been them.'

'Can't tell,' said Bill. 'Well – I seem to have had a lazy day. I've got some papers to read and then I suppose it will be supper time. There's going to be a fine moon tonight!'

'Just right for badgers,' Philip whispered to Jack. 'Like to come out and see if we can find any?'

'Rather,' said Jack. 'We can slip out when the others are in bed. Gussy always sleeps so soundly, he'll never hear!'

Supper time came. Cold ham, a salad, junket and cream. 'Just the right kind of meal,' said Philip. 'Why can't we have this kind of food at school?'

'Don't let's start up the subject of school meals *again*, Philip,' said his mother. 'You're yawning. Go to bed!'

'I think I will,' said Philip. 'Coming, Jack?'

Jack remembered that they had planned an outing in the moonlight, and he nodded. They might as well get a little sleep first. Gussy went up with them. The girls stayed down to finish their books and then went up too.

'I'll set my little alarm clock for eleven,' said Philip to Jack, in a low voice, not wanting Gussy to hear. 'I'll put it under my pillow and it won't wake anyone but me. Gosh, I'm sleepy.'

In ten minutes all the five children were fast asleep. Downstairs Bill and his wife sat listening to the radio. 'We'll hear the ten o'clock news and then go to bed,' said Bill.

But, just as the ten o'clock news was about to come on, there came a cautious tapping at the front door. Bill stiffened. Who was that? He looked at his wife, and she raised her eyebrows. Who could that be at this time of night?

Bill went quietly to the door. He didn't open it, but spoke with his mouth close to the crack.

'Who's there?'

'Oh, sir, Mrs Ellis has sent me down to beg you to come up to the farm,' said an anxious voice. 'It's her old aunt. She's fallen down and broken her hip. Can you come? Mrs Ellis is in such a way! She sent me to ask you, because the doctor's away.'

Bill opened the door. He saw a bent figure, wrapped round in a shawl. It must be Alice, the old woman who helped Mrs Ellis in the kitchen. 'Come in,' he said.

'No, sir, I'll be getting back,' said the old woman. 'You'll come, won't you?'

'Yes, we'll come,' said Bill. He shut the door and went back to tell his wife.

'It's a message from Mrs Ellis about the old aunt. Apparently she has fallen and broken her hip,' he said. 'Will you go, Allie? I'll take you there, of course, and then I must leave you and come back here, because of Gussy. But Mr Ellis will bring you back, unless you stay for the night.'

'Yes, I'd better go at once,' said Mrs Cunningham. 'Poor Mrs Ellis! Just what she was afraid might happen!'

She got her things on, and Bill and she went out of the door. 'It's not worth waking up the children and telling them,' he said. 'They're sound asleep. Anyway, I'll be back here in a few minutes' time.'

He shut the door quietly, made sure he had the key with him to open it when he came back, and then set off with his wife. What a wonderful moonlight night! Really, he would quite enjoy the walk!

11

Happenings in the night

The moonlight streamed down over the countryside as Bill and his wife set out. 'What a lovely night!' said Bill. 'As light as day, almost!'

They went up the tiny lane, hurrying as much as they could. 'I'll ask at the farm if Mr Ellis can bring you back,' Bill said. 'I won't stay even a minute. I'm worried about Gussy. I may get a glimpse of Madame Tatiosa and her companion – but I don't particularly want them to see *me*.'

They were passing a little copse of trees, a patch of dense black shadow in the surrounding moonlight. Bill and his wife walked by, not seeing a small movement in the shadows.

Then things happened very quickly indeed. Four shadows came from the copse of trees, running silently over the grass. Bill turned at a slight sound – but almost as he turned someone leapt on him and bore him to the ground.

Mrs Cunningham felt an arm round her, and a hand pressed over her mouth. She tried to scream, but only a small sound came from her.

'Don't struggle,' said a voice. 'And don't scream. We're not going to hurt you. We just want you out of the way for a short time.'

But Bill did struggle, of course. He knew what these men were after – Gussy! He groaned in anger at himself. This was a trick, of course! Old Aunt Naomi hadn't had a fall! There had been no real message from the farm. It was all a ruse to get them out of the house, so that it would be easy to kidnap Gussy.

Someone gagged his mouth by wrapping a cloth firmly round his face. He could hardly breathe! He wondered how his wife was getting on, but he could see and hear nothing. He stopped struggling when at last his arms were pinned behind him, and tied together with rope.

There was nothing he could do. It was four against two, and as they had been taken by surprise they were at a great disadvantage. Perhaps he would be able to undo the rope that bound him when his captors had gone to get Gussy. He might still prevent the kidnapping.

Mrs Cunningham was scared, and did her best to get away, but one man was quite sufficient to hold her and bind her hands and feet. She too was gagged so that she could not scream.

'We are sorry about this,' said a man's voice, quite politely. 'It is important to us to take the little Prince out of your hands. His country needs him. We shall not harm him in any way – and we have not harmed you either. We have merely put you to some inconvenience. Once we have the Prince one of us will come to untie you, if it is possible. If not – well, you will be found by some farm worker early in the morning.'

The men left Bill and his wife against a haystack, protected from the wind. One of them had gone through Bill's pockets first, and had taken out the key of the cottage.

Bill listened as the men went off. Were they gone? He rubbed his head against the ground trying to get off the cloth bound round his face. Was his wife all right?

He was furious with himself. To walk into a trap as easily as all that! The woman with the message must have been one of the gang, of course. No wonder she wouldn't come in. He should have been suspicious about that. An ordinary messenger would have waited for them and then walked to the farm in their company.

He remembered the 'ting' of the telephone that Jack said he had heard that afternoon. That must have been Madame Tatiosa or her companion telephoning to their headquarters to say that they knew where the Prince was, and requesting help to capture him. Another car must have come down that evening with other members of the gang. It all fitted in so well – but poor Bill saw the plot after it had been carried out, instead of before!

He wondered what was happening at Quarry Cottage.

He believed the man who had said that he was not going to harm the little Prince. All they wanted to do was to depose his uncle and set Gussy up in his place. Poor Gussy! He would be made to do all that the gang wanted, and his life would be very miserable.

Nothing was happening just then at Quarry Cottage. All the five children were fast asleep, and so was Kiki. The window of the boys' bedroom was shut, as Bill had ordered – but of what use was that when the enemy had the key to the front door!

Time crept on – and eleven o'clock came. Philip's alarm clock went off under his pillow, whirring in a muffled way that woke him up with a jump. At first he didn't know what the noise was, then he remembered.

'Eleven o'clock!' he thought, and slid his hand under his pillow to stop the alarm ringing. He sat up. Moonlight poured into the room, and made everything silvery. Just the night for badgers!

He padded across the room and shook Jack. 'Wake up! Eleven o'clock!' he whispered, right into his ear. He did not mean to wake Gussy, and have him clamouring to go with them! But Gussy was very sound asleep indeed. The moonlight streamed on to his face, and showed up the long lock of hair that had fallen as usual over his fore-head.

Kiki awoke as soon as the alarm went off. But she was used to muffled alarm clocks, and merely gave a little yawn, and stretched her wings. If the boys were going out, she was quite ready! Nothing would persuade her to be left behind.

The two boys dressed quickly in shorts, jerseys and rubber-soled shoes. They took a last glance at Gussy. His mouth was wide open again. Jack grinned as he remembered the bits of grass that Kiki had popped into it on Sugar-Loaf Hill.

They crept downstairs, pausing outside Bill's bedroom door to make sure all was quiet, and that Bill and his wife were asleep.

'Can't hear a thing,' whispered Jack. 'They must be *very* sound asleep! Not even a snore from Bill!'

This wasn't very surprising, of course, as Bill was at that moment struggling with his ropes as he lay in the shelter of the haystack.

'We'll go out the back way,' whispered Philip. 'The front door creaks a little. Don't bump into anything in the hall, for goodness' sake.'

Kiki was on Jack's shoulder, as quiet as the dormouse in Philip's pocket. She could always be depended on to keep silent when it was necessary. She knew quite well that the boys were trying not to be heard. She pecked Jack's ear affectionately, wondering what he was up to on this moonlight night.

The boys went out of the back door, and then stood still, debating which way to go.

'I think I'll come up to the little wood with you first,' said Jack. 'I might pop down to the quarry later, to hear the owls there, and see if I can watch them swooping on mice or rats.'

So they went silently to the wood on the east side of the cottage, making no noise in their rubber-soled shoes. They kept to the shadows of the hedges, afraid that someone might see them, even in this deserted spot. The moonlight was so very brilliant!

They came to the wood. Philip knew what type of place badgers would visit, and he led Jack to a hedge overshadowing a big bank.

'This is the sort of place to wait about in,' he said. 'Let's squeeze into that bush there.'

They crouched down in the black shadows. An owl suddenly hooted nearby, and Kiki at once hooted back, copying the long, quavering hoot exactly, and making Jack jump.

'Shut up, Kiki,' he whispered fiercely. 'You'll bring all the owls down on us with your hooting. Gosh, here comes the one you mimicked!'

An owl swooped by his head, and he ducked. So did Kiki! Kiki longed to hoot again. She loved puzzling any other bird.

She kept silent, half-sulky. The boys listened with their sharp ears, watching for any movement. Suddenly Jack gave Philip a nudge. A long, snake-like animal was hurrying by.

'Stoat,' whispered Philip in Jack's ear. 'And what's this? A hedgehog!'

The hedgehog was curious about the black shadows sitting under the bush. He came fearlessly up to investigate. Philip put out his hand slowly, and the hedgehog sniffed it over. Jack quite expected to see him climb on to Philip's knee! No creature was ever afraid of him.

But the hedgehog was hungry and he ran off to find the slugs he liked best. The boys thought he went along as if he was a little clockwork animal. They waited for the next night creature to appear.

And this time it was a badger! It really was. Philip drew in his breath sharply. He had hardly hoped to see one so soon. It was a biggish creature, with a curiously striped black and white face. It stood absolutely still in the moonlight, sniffing, wondering if it could smell a danger-smell – a smell of humans?

But the wind blew from the badger to the boys, and he could smell nothing. He could hardly be seen as he stood in the full moonlight, because the black and white stripes down his face were so exactly like the black and white shadows of this moonlit night.

'Perfect camouflage!' whispered Philip, and Jack nodded. Then he nudged Philip. Something else was coming.

'*Young* badgers!' thought Philip, in delight. 'A family party – yes, there's mother badger at the back. What a bit of luck!'

The young badgers were skittish little bear-like things. They began to play about, and the two boys watched their curious games, quite fascinated.

The little badgers began to bounce. They really *did* bounce, on all four legs, jumping up and down in the same place, looking like fat, furry balls. They bounced at one another! One knocked another over, but in a flash he turned a somersault, came up under the first badger and knocked *him* over!

This head-over-heels game seemed a favourite one, and the young badgers played it for some time. Then the parents gave a little call, and went off into the wood; the young ones stopped their game and followed.

Jack gave a little laugh. 'What an amusing sight! I've never seen animals play *that* game before! Do all badgers turn head-over-heels like that?'

'I've heard so,' said Philip. 'A keeper once told me that a grown badger will spring traps that way – he just turns himself head-over-heels on the trap, sets it off, and then takes the bait! All he loses is a few hairs off his back.'

An owl hooted again, some way off. It was a tawny owl calling. Then there was a screech from a barn owl. Kiki stirred on Jack's shoulders. She was longing to do a bit of hooting and screeching herself!

'I think I'll go back now,' said Philip, getting up. 'I'd like to stay and watch for a few more creatures to come by, but I'm afraid I shall fall asleep. You coming, Jack?'

'Well – I rather think I'll go and wander round that quarry a bit,' said Jack. 'I'd like to see what owls are there – and I'd like to give old Kiki the chance of calling them, to see if she really can bring them to her. I know she's longing to try. Aren't you, Kiki, old bird?'

Kiki muttered something into his ear, afraid of speaking out loud. Jack got up and stretched. 'Well, you get to bed, and I'll come when I'm ready,' he said. 'I'll be about half an hour, I expect. Don't be surprised if you hear thousands of hoots in a little while, once Kiki gets going!'

Philip went back to the cottage, and Jack made his way to the quarry. Little did they guess what a shock they were both going to get in the next ten minutes!

12

Capture!

Philip made his way to the back door of the cottage, but just as he was about to go in, he stopped. What noise was that? It sounded like someone going to the front door – someone tiptoeing up the path, surely?

The boy hesitated. Could it be someone after Gussy? He'd better warn Bill then – go in and wake him. He tip-toed quietly through the back door, into the hall and up the stairs. He stopped at the top and looked back, hearing a small sound.

The front door was opening quietly, but with the little creak it always gave. Then a torch was flashed on and off very quickly. Yes – somebody *was* getting in.

Philip yelled at the top of his voice. 'Bill! BILL! BILL! Wake up, Bill. There's someone getting in.'

He was standing just outside the girls' door as he yelled, and they woke up at once. Gracious! – who was shouting like that?

'Someone's getting in. Quick, Bill, quick!' shouted

Philip again, wondering why there was no answering shout from Bill's room nearby.

The girls' door opened and Dinah looked out, scared. 'What is it? Who is it? Where's Bill?'

'Keep where you are,' said a voice suddenly, and a torch was flashed on to the three of them, for Lucy-Ann had now appeared, trembling.

Philip pushed the girls violently, and they almost fell into their bedroom. Then he rushed into Bill's room, yelling again. 'BILL! Do wake up!'

The moonlight showed him a completely empty bed – a bed not even slept in! Then where was Bill? And his mother – where was *she*? Philip was astounded.

Gussy was now awake, up in the attic bedroom. He sat up, bewildered. What was all this shouting? He suddenly noticed that Jack and Philip were not in their beds, and he leapt out of his, afraid.

Downstairs, in Bill's bedroom, Philip was still yelling. Bill *must* be somewhere about – but where? 'Bill! I say, BILL!'

A torch flashed into the room, and two figures loomed up by the door.

'You won't find Bill,' said a voice. 'Or his wife either. We've got them. And now we want the Prince Aloysius. We do not intend to harm him in any way – but he must come with us. His country needs him.'

'What have you done with my mother?' demanded Philip, fiercely. 'I'll get the police! What do you think you're doing, capturing people, and coming after the Prince! You can't do that kind of thing in Britain!'

'Oh yes, we can,' said the foreign voice, smoothly, and the man stepped into the moonlight. Philip saw that it was the man who had come with the woman that afternoon. Behind him were other people – how many? Philip wished that Jack was with him. One boy wasn't much against all these people. He didn't count Gussy as a boy!

One of the men behind called out something in a language that Philip didn't understand, and received a sharp order in return. There was the sound of feet on the stairs leading up to the attic bedroom. They were after Gussy, who had done quite the wrong thing, and had appeared at the top in the bright moonlight! He had been seen at once, of course.

Gussy fled into the bedroom, slammed the door and locked it. He leaned against it, trembling. Then he ran to the window. Could he get out?

No. Gussy was no climber, and although Jack and Philip would certainly have had a shot at clambering down the creeper, Gussy was afraid he might fall.

'Unlock this door!' cried a voice, but Gussy did not obey. Then two of the men flung themselves against it, and it broke down easily. They clambered over the broken panels and went to Gussy. He screamed.

One of the men bowed to him. 'Your Highness, we have not come to harm you. We have come to take you back to Tauri-Hessia to be crowned King in the place of your uncle. He is not liked, your uncle. The people want you instead.'

'It's a lie!' shouted Gussy, trembling. 'I've been told all about it. My uncle is too strong a ruler for you, and you want a boy instead who will do as he is told. I will not come!'

All this was said in his own language, so that the girls, listening fearfully in their room below, did not understand a word. Philip pushed by the men at the door of Bill's room and ran up to Gussy.

'Look here,' he said fiercely to the two men there. 'You know that the British Government *and* your own Government won't let you make Gussy King. You'll get into trouble with our Government, you know. You'll be clapped into prison either here or in your own country.'

The men, joined by the other two below, had a quick conference. Philip didn't understand a word. Then the tall man with the eyeglass bowed slightly to Philip.

'You too will come with us,' he said, 'and the other children as well. You will – er – be companions for our little Prince – and we do not think your Government will be *too* angry when they know we hold you also!'

'Oh! So you think you'll take us and make us a kind of hostage, do you?' said Philip, quite beside himself with rage. 'You think you can bargain with our Government just because you'll hold us prisoners! My word, you don't know the British people. You'll be sorry for this! Holding us to ransom! I never heard such a fatheaded idea in my life. You aren't living in the Middle Ages, you know!'

The man heard him out to the end, quite politely. Then he made a motion with his hand, and two of the men pounced on Philip and Gussy and held them in such a vice-like grip that it was quite hopeless to get away.

'Run, you two – run!' yelled Philip at the top of his voice, hoping that Dinah and Lucy-Ann would have the sense to rush into the woods and get away. But although they did manage to tear downstairs, they found a man in the hall, and he was quite able to hold the two kicking, yelling girls until yet another fellow came to his help.

Sharp orders were given by the man with the eyeglass, who seemed to be in command. One man detached himself and went upstairs. He came down with an assortment of clothes for the girls and Gussy, who was, of course, still in his beautiful silk pyjamas. The girls were in pyjamas and dressing gowns, but had no slippers on. The man was sent back to fetch shoes.

'Where's Bill?' said Lucy-Ann, with chattering teeth. 'I want Bill. What have they done with him? And where's Aunt Allie?'

'Don't be frightened,' said the man with the eyeglass, patting her. 'We shall treat you very kindly. We shall not hurt you. It will be nice for the little Prince Aloysius to have his friends with him. You will have a fine time in Tauri-Hessia.'

Lucy-Ann suddenly realized that Jack was missing.

She looked round wildly for him. 'Where's Jack? What have you done with Jack?'

'Ah, yes – there was another boy. I remember now,' said the chief man. 'Where is he?'

'Out bird-watching,' said Philip, sullenly. His only hope now was that Jack would see and hear this disturbance and go to fetch help before they were all whisked away. He had given up struggling. What was the use? He would only get hurt, and he could see that if the girls were going to be captured, he certainly must go with them to look after them as best he could.

'Bird-watching! At this time of night!' said the man. 'What strange habits you Britishers have! We will not wait for this boy Jack. We do not need him.'

They opened the front door again, and pushed the four children out in front of them, holding their arms tightly.

'It is of no use to scream,' said the chief, still very politely.

'There is no one to hear you – and we should gag you if you did scream.'

'Philip – what shall we do?' asked Dinah, scarlet with rage at being captured like this.

'Nothing,' said Philip. 'Just – er – hope for the best.'

Dinah guessed what he meant. Perhaps even at this very minute Jack was bringing help!

Lucy-Ann stumbled along miserably in her dressing gown. She had been allowed to put on her shoes, and so had the others. She was worried about Bill and her aunt, and very *very* worried about Jack. Would she be taken off to Tauri-Hessia and have to leave Jack for months and months? Where *was* Jack?

Jack was down in the quarry with Kiki. He had found plenty of owls hooting and screeching there, for, as the old farm hand had said, it was a wonderful hunting place for owls of all kinds.

Kiki had been having the time of her life. She had hooted and screeched and twitted, and had brought a crowd of owls almost down to Jack's shoulders. One owl, a barn owl, had screeched deafeningly in his ear, and had struck him with a wing.

Jack decided that he was too easily seen where he stood. He must get under a bush somewhere, or else the next owl might scratch his face with a sharp talon or two!

He moved to the other side of the quarry and made his way to a big hedge there. As he drew near, the moonlight glinted on something under the hedge. Something that shone brightly. Jack stopped. What could it be?

He went cautiously forward, and saw that something dark and long and very big was under the tall hedge, as close to it as possible. The moonlight caught its polished surface here and there.

'Gosh! It's a car!' said Jack, in the greatest astonishment. 'A car exactly like the one the couple have at the farm – it must be the same one. What's it doing here?'

He went over to it. It was empty. Nobody was in it at all. The key had been taken out so that it could not be driven away.

'Has somebody parked it here to go and spy round Quarry Cottage?' wondered Jack. He went to the back of the car. It had an enormous luggage boot. Jack opened it and peered inside. It was empty except for an extra inner tube and a few tools.

Kiki hooted again, and an owl answered her. 'Be quiet now, Kiki,' said Jack. 'We've got to do a bit of spying. We'll creep back to Quarry Cottage and see if there's anyone snooping round there.'

But before he could do that, he heard the sound of footsteps coming into the quarry, and he dived into some bushes.

The footsteps made quite a lot of noise, because there were eight people coming into the deserted quarry, where the car had been parked. Jack peered out of his bush and saw, to his great alarm, that Philip, Dinah, Lucy-Ann and Gussy were all being held very firmly indeed! He stared, bewildered, unable to think what to do.

Kiki suddenly screeched – but it was not an owl screech, it was a real parrot screech – and Philip recognized it at once. It was Kiki! Then Jack must be somewhere in the quarry still!

He gave a shout. 'They're taking us away! Tell Bill!'

The man holding him gave him a shove. 'You were

told not to shout! What's the use of shouting here? There's no one to hear you!'

But there was, of course. There was Jack. But what was Jack to DO?

13

The extra passenger

Jack stared in distress at the four children being bundled into the car – Philip and Dinah at the back with three men, and Gussy and Lucy-Ann in front with the driver. What a crowd! If anyone saw the car going along with such a number of people in, surely it would be noticed and stopped?

'Yes, it would,' thought Jack, 'so that means they can't be going very far – they will arrive at their destination before daylight. Are they going to take them to some hiding place fairly near then? Why in the world have they got Philip and the girls as well as Gussy?'

Everyone was now in the car. The doors were shut as quietly as possible. The engine was started up – and just at that very moment Jack had an idea!

He ran, crouching, to the back of the car. He hadn't had time to shut the luggage boot properly when he had opened it to look inside. Could he get into it before the car drove off? It was such a fine big one.

The car began to move very slowly out of the quarry, bumping over rough places. Jack flung himself at the back of it, and clambered up on to the luggage boot. It swung right open, and Jack half-fell into it. Kiki was astounded, and flew off his shoulder at once. Jack stared at her anxiously. He dared not call her back.

But, as soon as she saw Jack settled in the boot, she flew down again, and found his shoulder. She talked solemnly into his ear, in a very low voice, trying to tell him in parrot language that she thought these goings-on were extremely peculiar, but that so long as Jack approved of them, she did too – and she was coming with him, even in this dark, smelly car boot!

Jack felt comforted to have her. He puzzled over everything. Where was Bill? And Aunt Allie? How was it these fellows had been able to get into Quarry Cottage so easily and capture everyone? But what had they done with Bill? Was he lying knocked out in the cottage? Ought Jack to have gone to see, instead of climbing into the boot?

The car had now gathered speed and was going down country lanes very fast. It drew up once, at some dark little house, where a man came out. There was another car there and one of the men in the first car thankfully got out and went to the second car. This went on ahead, as if guiding the other. Jack was glad. He didn't want bright head lights behind him, showing him sitting in the boot!

'I ought to close the boot and shut myself in. But suppose I can't get it open again?' he thought. 'I simply *must* see what place they're taking the others to. If I can do that, I can soon raise the alarm, have the place surrounded, and everyone rescued! I hope no one sees me here.'

Another hour's run in the smooth-running powerful car – then it stopped. There was a sharp exchange of words, a light flashed, and a gate creaked open.

'Hallo! We're here already, wherever that may be!' thought Jack. 'Had I better get out now, while the car has stopped? Blow – it's too late. They're going on again.'

The car bumped over a dark field. And then suddenly a strange, extraordinarily loud noise started up not far ahead. Jack jumped violently, and Kiki gave a loud screech, which fortunately couldn't possibly be heard in the enormous noise going on.

'An aeroplane!' said Jack. 'So *that's* what they've planned. They're going off to Tauri-Hessia! They must be. And they'll hide Gussy somewhere till their plans are all ready, and the girls and Philip with him. Nobody will know where they are.'

He felt the car come to a stop with a bump. He crawled out of the boot at once, and ran to a big shape looming up nearby. It was a lorry. Jack crouched beside it, watching.

He saw an aeroplane not far off, its propellers whirring. It hadn't all its lights on yet, but men were round it with lamps. It was obviously soon going to take off.

What was this place? A private airfield? Jack had no idea at all. He watched all the passengers in the big black car tumbling out, one after the other. He thought he heard Lucy-Ann crying, and his heart sank. She would hate all this! She wasn't tough, like Dinah. Where would she be tomorrow?

Everyone was hurried towards the plane. Jack left his hiding place and hurried too. He had had another idea! Could he hide in the plane? He had hidden in the car, and no one had suspected it. Would there be any place to hide in the plane?

He thought of the planes he had flown in. The luggage-space would be the only place. There probably wouldn't be much there. It was a risk, but he'd take it. If he was discovered, well, at least he'd be with the others.

'But I *mustn't* be discovered!' he thought desperately. 'If I am I'll be hidden away somewhere too – and I simply *must* find out where the others are being taken, so that I can somehow get word to Bill.'

Kiki came to his help, quite unexpectedly. She didn't see why she shouldn't talk to the others, whose voices she had recognized as soon as she heard them getting out of the car. She left Jack's shoulder and flew towards Lucy-Ann.

'Pop goes the weasel!' she cried. 'God save the King! Send for the doctor!'

The four children in front turned round in utter amazement. 'Kiki! KIKI! How did *you* get here?'

The men pushing them forward stopped at once. They had no idea that Kiki was only a parrot, and had not even spotted her in the darkness. They thought she must be someone coming after the children, on the airfield, someone quite unexpected, who had followed them!

Orders were shouted. Lamps flashed here and there. Kiki was frightened and flew back to Jack.

'Wipe your feet!' she called, much to the amazement of the men with the lamps.

Jack ran round the other side of the lorry, for the men were coming too near him. Then he saw his chance. Everyone's attention was on the men who were searching the field with lamps. Nobody was watching the plane.

Jack ran to it in the darkness, stumbling as he went. Thank goodness the moon had conveniently gone behind a remarkably black cloud! He felt a drop of rain. Perhaps the moon wouldn't come out till he was safely in the plane.

He reached the plane, and thankfully saw the steps up to it. He ran up and found himself in the plane. No one was there. He groped his way to the back, where he hoped to find the luggage-space. He felt something that was shaped like a crate. Yes – this must be where they put the luggage! He felt round again, and came across a box. It had a lid, and he lifted it up, hoping that the box was empty.

It wasn't. It was full of something soft, that might be

clothes, or material of some kind. It felt like silk. Jack pulled most of it out and stuffed in into a corner, behind the big crate.

Then he hurriedly got into the box and pulled the lid down. Only just in time! Kiki was with him, of course, silent and astonished. Jack had tapped her beak to tell her she must be absolutely quiet.

He heard the sound of voices and the noise of feet going up the steps into the plane. He heard shouts, and bangs and whirs. The propellers, which had stopped, were started up again, and the aeroplane shook violently.

The wheels bumped very slowly over the field and then the bumping stopped.

'We've taken off,' thought Jack, thankfully. 'And I'm here with the others, though they don't know it. Now will my luck hold? Shall I get to wherever they're going without being discovered? I do hope so! If only I can find out where they will be hidden, things will be easy.'

It was uncomfortable in the box, but as Jack had left some of the soft material at the bottom, at least he had something soft to crouch on. Kiki didn't like it at all. She grumbled in his ear, and then suddenly produced a tremendous sneeze.

It sounded very loud indeed to Jack. He sat as quiet as a mouse, waiting for someone to come and look round the luggage-space. But nobody did. The noise of the engines was too loud for Kiki's sneeze to be heard. It was a real sneeze, not a pretend one, and Kiki was just as surprised as Jack was when it came.

The children in the front of the plane talked in low voices, sure that the engines would drown what they were saying. It seemed queer to be sitting in a plane dressed in night clothes – all but Philip, of course.

'*Was* that Kiki we heard out on the field?' said Lucy-Ann. 'It must have been. I'm sure I heard "Pop goes the weasel"!'

'I believe it was,' said Philip. 'I wouldn't be surprised if old Jack hung on to that car somehow. After all, we know he was in that quarry – he probably saw what was happening, and managed to hang on behind somewhere.'

'I wish he was with us now,' sighed Lucy-Ann. 'I shan't like being without him. Where are we going, I wonder? To some horrid old castle – or perhaps a palace? Gussy, have you got a palace?'

'Yes,' said Gussy. 'But only a small one. We shan't go there, because the people know me. They would see me. I have heard these men talking, and they do not want me to be seen yet. First they must deal with my uncle. I hope they will not kill him. He is nice, my uncle.'

'I sincerely hope they *won't* do anything of the sort,' said Philip. 'You'd *have* to be King then, Gussy. How I'd hate to be a King! Always having to be on my best behaviour, never to lose my temper or do a thing that was wrong or impolite, having to be nice to people I hated, and . . .'

'Why isn't your father King?' asked Dinah. 'Why are *you* the heir to the throne?'

'My father is dead,' said Gussy. 'There is only my mother, and in our country women are not allowed to rule. So one day I must be King. I shall like it.'

'Well – you like ordering people about, and showing off,' said Dinah. 'So I suppose it'll suit you. But I can't say you're my idea of a King. Oh dear – I wish this hadn't happened. All our Easter hols spoiled!'

'I hate all this,' said Lucy-Ann, dismally. 'I'm cold, and now I'm sleepy.'

'Cuddle up to me,' said Dinah. 'After all, it's the middle of the night, so we *ought* to feel sleepy. I do too. Let's go to sleep. It will make the night seem shorter.'

'I could go to sleep at once if I didn't keep thinking of Bill and Aunt Allie,' said Lucy-Ann, shutting her eyes, and getting close to Dinah for warmth. 'I keep on thinking about – about – I keep on . . .'

Philip smiled at Dinah over Lucy-Ann's head. She was asleep already, in spite of her 'thinking'. Poor Lucy-Ann – she fell into adventures as readily as the others, but she didn't enjoy them nearly so much!

Jack fell into an uncomfortable sleep too, in his box in the luggage-space. Kiki tucked her head under her wing and slept peacefully. The plane went on and on in the night, through a rain-storm, and then out into clear weather again, with a moon still bright in the sky.

None of the children saw that it was flying over the

brilliant, moonlit sea. None of them gazed down to see the towns that looked like toy villages far below. The engines droned on and on, and the rhythm lulled the sleepers for mile upon mile.

And then the plane began to circle over a small airfield. It had arrived! Philip woke in a hurry and shook the girls. Gussy woke too and looked down from the window.

'Tauri-Hessia!' he said, proudly. 'My country, Tauri-Hessia!'

14

Jack is on his own

The sun was up, just above the horizon, when the plane landed gently on the runway. The sky was golden, and in the distance small whitewashed houses gleamed brightly.

Jack awoke when the engines stopped. He lifted up the lid of his box slightly, listening. Had they arrived? Then he heard Gussy's voice. 'Tauri-Hessia!'

'So we've arrived,' thought Jack. 'Now – what do I do next? It's daylight – though I should guess it's only just sunrise.'

The four children in front were hustled out. The little airfield was completely deserted except for a few mechanics. A large car stood waiting. The children were pushed into it without a moment's pause. Obviously they were to be hurried somewhere secret as fast as possible.

Jack got out of the box and made his way cautiously to a window. He saw the children just below, getting into a big car. The man with the eyeglass appeared to be in command, and gave an order to the chauffeur as he got in. The man was holding open the door and bowed. He saluted too, and repeated something after the man with the eyeglass.

'Borken!'

Then he got into the driving-seat and drove swiftly off the field to a large gate in the distance.

'Borken!' said Jack to himself. 'Now would that be the name of a place – or just a Hessian word for "Thank you" or something? Well – they've gone. Kiki, you and I are on our own in a strange land whose language we don't know. And we have only got a few English coins in our pocket – so what do you suppose is the best thing to do?'

'Send for the doctor,' said Kiki, putting up her crest and looking very wise. 'Send for the doctor. Put the kettle on.'

Jack went on looking out of the window. It seemed to him that everyone had walked off to a little wooden building at one end of the airfield – to get refreshments, perhaps? Jack felt that he would like some too!

He went cautiously into the other part of the plane. Not a soul was there. In fact, not a soul was to be seen anywhere, even on the field or in the distance.

'I think the time has come for us to go, Kiki,' said Jack. 'Ready for a sprint? I hardly think we'll get away without being noticed – but at any rate we'll have a good start, if the men have to come from that wooden building right over there.'

He went to the landing steps and ran down them.

Then he sprinted at top speed across the field to the entrance. Nothing happened for a minute or two, and then two men appeared at the door of the distant building. They shouted loudly, and then began to run after Jack.

But he had a wonderful start, and the men gave up almost at once, and returned to the building. 'Just a boy longing for a close look at an aeroplane!' they said to one another.

Jack ran out of the entrance and found himself on a wide, deserted road. No one was in sight. He could not even see any houses. This must be a very lonely airfield! He began to walk along the road, Kiki on his shoulder. He was very hungry indeed now.

'Why isn't anyone about?' he thought. 'Not a car to be seen so I can't get a lift. I wonder where the others are by now? Wish I was with them!'

He suddenly remembered that it was very early in the morning. Of course no one would be about yet. The sun had only just risen. Possibly he might meet a workman or two soon.

He met a man cycling along the road after a while and held up his hand to stop him. The man put one foot on the road, and stopped his bicycle.

'Eglinoota?' he said. At least, that is what it sounded like to Jack. He looked astonished to see Kiki.

'I'm English,' said Jack, trying to speak slowly and clearly. 'Where is the police station?'

'Eglinoota?' said the man again, looking bewildered. 'Oota? Oota?'

'Parp-parp,' said Kiki, suddenly. 'Parp-parp!' It sounded exactly like the hooter of a car! Jack laughed.

'Did you think the man kept saying "hooter"?' he asked Kiki. 'Well, he wasn't. Goodness knows what he was saying! I wish I knew what "food" was in the Hessian language!'

'Powkepotoplink?' said the man, trying again. He pointed to the parrot. 'Powkepotoplink? Ai, ai!'

He suddenly took out a notebook and a pencil and began drawing something on a page. Jack wondered what it was. The man tore out the page and gave it to him.

The drawing looked like a small map showing various roads. There was something that looked like a pond also, and something else that looked like a church spire. At the bottom of the map the man had drawn what looked like a tent. He jabbed at it with his pencil.

'Powkepotoplink,' he said again, very loudly, as if that might help Jack to understand.

'Plink-plonk, plink-plonk,' said Kiki, at once, and went off into a cackle of laughter. The man looked at her in admiration. He undid a bag and took out a small sugared cake. He presented it to Kiki, who took it with her right foot, making a sudden clucking noise like a hen.

Jack looked at it with hungry eyes and the man noticed the look. He delved in his bag again and brought out an enormously thick sandwich with some kind of bright red meat in it. He presented this to Jack, who was thrilled.

'Thank you,' said the boy. 'Thank you very much.'

'Cheepalikkle,' said the man, incomprehensibly, and rode off, waving. Jack walked on, munching the huge sandwich. Kiki put out her parrot-tongue and licked the cake. She didn't like it and gave it to Jack. In return he gave her some of her favourite sunflower seeds, of which he always kept a supply in his pocket. She sat happily on his shoulder, cracking them.

Jack looked at the map. What did it mean? Why had that man drawn it? He must have thought there was some particular place Jack wanted to go to – but Jack himself didn't know of any place in Tauri-Hessia that he wanted to find, except the place where the others had gone. And that might be Borken and it might not. Borken might mean anything in this unknown Hessian language!

He walked on and on for miles, feeling much better for the sandwich. He decided that he must look for a police station if ever he came to the end of this wide, deserted road. It looked as if it had only been built to lead to the airfield! Except for the man on the bicycle he met nobody at all.

But at last he saw houses in the distance. Ah – he was coming to a village – no, a town, because as he came nearer he saw that it was far too big to be called a village.

'If I could just find somebody who spoke English, it would be such a help,' thought Jack. 'I could ask for a police station then, and get a telegram – or a cable – sent to Bill. I wish he'd come out here and help. I wonder what happened to him. I bet those fellows knocked him out.'

He came into the town and looked around him with interest. The shops were small and dark, the houses were whitewashed or pink-washed, and seemed to run to curls and squiggles and much decoration – rather 'fretworky', Jack decided. Curly roofs, squiggly bits of woodwork here and there, and windows whose sills were covered with decorated flower boxes.

The people looked like farmers and were dressed in bright, simple clothes. No woman wore a hat, but many wore shawls. The men wore rather tight trousers, and had some kind of sash round their waists. Their waistcoats were gaily embroidered, and somehow they reminded Jack of bull fighters though he didn't quite know why.

The children were very thin, and simply dressed. Even the little girls wore long, rather raggedy skirts, and the boys wore tight trousers like their fathers but had no embroidered waistcoats. Instead they had very bright red, blue or yellow shirts.

They soon saw Jack, and ran to him. The parrot fascinated them.

'Powke, powke!' they yelled, pointing at Kiki, who was delighted at being the centre of attention. She put up her crest and lowered it, and even did a little hoppity dance on Jack's shoulder.

'Powke – that must mean parrot,' thought Jack. 'Hey, you kids – where's the police station?'

They didn't understand a word, of course. They followed Jack, talking together, still entertained by Kiki, who was showing off tremendously.

Then a small boy with a little wooden gun ran up. He pointed it at Jack, and shouted 'Pop-pop-pop!'

That was quite enough for Kiki. She stood up on her toes and shouted at the top of her voice. 'Pop! POP! BANG-BANG-BANG! Pop goes the weasel! Powke, powke, powke.'

There was an awed silence after this effort of Kiki's. Everyone stared, still trotting after Jack.

Kiki went off into one of her idiotic bouts of laughter, and the children all began to laugh too.

'Wipe your feet, blow your nose!' shouted Kiki, and then made a noise like an express train in a tunnel.

This made a tremendous impression. The children fell back a little, startled. But they soon caught up again, yelling 'Powke, powke, powke', and soon the crowd was considerably bigger, and Jack began to feel like the Pied Piper of Hamelin with so many children following him.

Then an official-looking person stopped him at a crossroads, and addressed him quite sternly, pointing to the crowd that had now gathered round him. Jack didn't understand a word.

'I am English,' he said. 'English. You speak English? Yes? No?'

'Ha! Ingleeeeesh!' said the person, and took out a

black notebook which immediately told Jack what he was. Of course – a Hessian policeman!

'You speak English?' said Jack, hopefully.

The policeman rattled off something at him, and held out his hand. He still had the notebook in the other one. Jack hadn't the faintest idea what he wanted. He shook his head, puzzled. The policeman grew annoyed. He slapped his hand with the notebook and shouted again.

Jack shook his head once more. Kiki shouted back at the policeman. 'Pop goes the weasel, put the kettle on, POP!'

All the children laughed. There were a good many grown-ups around now, watching. One suddenly put his hand into his pocket and drew out a worn, doubled-over card. He showed it to Jack, and made him understand that that was what the policeman was asking him for.

Jack saw that it was a kind of passport or identity card. He hadn't got one on him, of course, so once more he shook his head. Kiki shook hers, too, and the children roared.

The policeman shut his notebook with a snap and put his hand on Jack's shoulder. He fired a sentence at him in sharp Hessian and pushed him in front of him smartly.

'Now where do we go?' thought Jack. 'What a colour-ful policeman – blue trousers, red shirt, blue sash, an imposing kind of flower-pot helmet – really!'

But he didn't think things were quite so happy when he saw where the policeman was taking him. There was no doubt about it at all. It was a police station, a small, square, whitewashed place, sober-looking and severe, with a good many more stern-faced policemen standing about.

'Look here! You can't put *me* into prison!' cried Jack, struggling away. 'I've done nothing wrong! You let me go!'

15

The map comes in useful

Jack was pushed firmly into a small, square room with one bench in it against the wall. He was made to sit down on this, and the policeman went to report at a big, untidy desk. He spoke very quickly, and it all sounded like a lot of Double Dutch to Jack.

It did to Kiki too, and she sat on Jack's shoulder and sent out such a stream of unending nonsense that every policeman in the place stared in admiration.

Nobody was standing in Jack's way to the door. He looked at it. He thought he would make a dash for freedom, and try to get away from these awkward policemen. He was half-afraid he might be locked up for weeks. Perhaps they thought he was a beggar or a tramp? Perhaps it was a great crime not to have some kind of card to say who he was?

He saw his chance, when nobody was looking at him, and raced for the door. He was down the steps and into the street before a policeman stirred! He heard shouts behind him but he didn't look back. Down the dusty street he ran at top speed, turned a corner, ran down an alley, and came to a big door.

He ran inside and looked round. No one was there. A squawk attracted his attention, and made Kiki look round in interest. Jack saw a parrot in a cage, a very colourful one with blue and green and yellow feathers.

Kiki flew to the cage and stood on the top. She bent her head down and looked inside excitedly. Another parrot!

'How-do-you-do, how-do-you-do!' said Kiki. 'Good morning, good night! Pop goes the weasel!'

The other parrot gave another squawk. It seemed rather scared. Then Jack heard the sound of footsteps, and before he could move, a voice spoke – a gentle voice, soft and kind.

A girl stood there, aged about twelve. She was beautifully dressed in bright silks, and her long dark hair was woven in and out with bright ribbons. She stared at Jack in surprise.

'Eglinoota?' said the girl. 'Oota?'

Jack wished he knew what this 'oota' word meant. He really didn't know what to say. He pointed to the parrots and smiled cheerfully. 'Powke, powke!' he said. The girl looked at the two parrots and laughed.

Then, to his delight, she slowly spoke a few words in English. 'Where – you – go?' she said. 'You – English – yes?'

Jack fished out the bit of paper the man on the bicycle had drawn him. It would look as if he really *was* going somewhere, if he showed her that! She took it and nodded her head.

'Come,' she said, and took him to the door.

'Listen – do you know anyone who speaks English well?' asked Jack, eagerly. The girl didn't understand, though he repeated it several times. Then she heard a voice from somewhere in the house, and she gave him a push, pointing down an alley, and then to the right. Jack thanked her, called Kiki and went out. He ran down the alley and came to the end. Then he turned to the right and went quickly along a narrow, dusty street with high walls each side.

He stopped at the end and looked at his map. He supposed he might as well follow it. Obviously the bicyclist must have had some reason for drawing it. It might lead somewhere useful!

In front of him was what would be, in England, a village green. But this green was parched and dusty, and three skinny hens wandered over it looking thoroughly miserable. At the side was a big round pond in which dozens of small children were paddling. Jack looked at his map again.

'Ah – the pond! Yes, I must be on the right road. I'll go down here, and see if I can spot the thing that looks like a church tower.'

He went on for some way without seeing anything like

a church tower. At last he stopped a kindly-looking old woman and showed her the map. He pointed to the drawing that looked like a church.

She nodded her head at once. She took his arm and pointed across a field. There was a path there. It led upwards towards a hill. On the hill Jack saw a building with a great tower. He couldn't imagine what it was, unless it was a Tauri-Hessian church.

He went on again, over the field and up to the tower. He looked at the map again – it showed a winding road from the tower and this road led to the drawing on the map that looked rather like a tent. Jack looked up from the map and recognized the winding road, going down the other side of the hill on which the tower stood. But what could the tent-like drawing be?

An old man sat on a bench, dozing. Jack went cautiously up to him and sat down. The old man opened an eye, saw the parrot and sat up at once.

'Good. He's awake,' thought Jack, and pushed the map in front of him, pointing to the tent-like drawing, and trying to make the man understand that he wanted to get there.

'Ahhhh!' said the old fellow, in a hoarse voice. 'Pikkatioratyforg. Ahhhhhh!'

'Very helpful!' thought Jack. The old man got up and tottered a little way down the path. Then he pointed with his stick.

'Surkytalar,' he said. 'Surky.'

'Surky,' repeated Jack, and looked where he was pointing. Then he stared hard. He knew why the bicyclist had drawn the tent now! In a big field were crowds of tents and vans! It must be a circus of some kind – a travelling circus!

'Of course! Surky – he means circus,' thought Jack. 'It's a circus. That's why that fellow on the bike directed me there. He thought I wanted the circus – thought I was trying to make my way to it, because I'd got a talking parrot. Well, well, well! I've solved *that* puzzle!'

He thanked the old man and thought he might as well make his way to the circus. Somebody there might possibly speak English. Circus people knew all kinds of languages. Anyway they were usually kindly folk, they might give him a meal and help him a bit.

So Jack, suddenly feeling very hungry again, went down the long winding road to the field where the circus was.

It took him about half an hour to reach it and when he got there he saw that it was packing up to move on. The tents were being taken down, horses were being put into some of the vans and there was a great deal of shouting and noise.

Jack leaned over the gate. A boy came by, carrying a load of boxes that looked very heavy. As he passed, the pile toppled over, and he dropped about four of them. Jack leapt over the gate and went to help.

The boy was about his own age, swarthy and black-eyed. He grinned at Jack, and said something he couldn't understand. He said it again, in another language. Still Jack didn't understand.

'Merci beaucoup,' said the boy, trying again this time in French. Ah – Jack understood that!

'Ce n'est rien!' he answered. The boy looked at Kiki and rattled off something in French again, asking Jack if he was a circus boy and had come to ask for a job there.

Jack answered as best he could, for his French was not really very good. 'I should like a job,' said Jack, in French. 'Better still, I should like a meal!'

'Come with me then,' said the boy, again in French, and Jack followed him to a van. A woman sat there, peeling potatoes.

'Ma!' said the boy, in English. 'Here's a hungry kid. Got anything for him?'

Jack stared at the boy in astonishment. Why, he was speaking English! 'Hey!' said Jack, 'why didn't you speak English before? I'm English!'

'My dad's English', said the boy, grinning. 'My ma's Spanish. We don't mind what language we speak, really. We've picked them all up in our wanderings around. Ma, give this boy something to eat. Do you think he can get a job with us? Where do you want to go?' he asked Jack.

'Well – is there a place called Borken anywhere about?' asked Jack, hopefully.

'Borken! Yes, we're on the way there,' said the boy, and

Jack felt suddenly cheerful. 'It's a big town, and outside there's the Castle of Borken on a hill.'

Jack drank all this in. A castle – would that be where the others had been taken? This *was* a bit of luck after all his set-backs. He would certainly go with this travelling circus if they would have him.

Ma gave him a meal. It was very rich and rather greasy, but Jack enjoyed it because he was so hungry. Then Ma said something commanding in Spanish and the boy nodded.

'Got to take you to the Boss,' he said. 'And let him look you over. Got anyone to speak for you? Anyone's name to give? The Boss will give you up to the police if you've run away from any kind of trouble.'

'No, I don't know anyone here who will speak for me,' said Jack, anxiously. 'I just want to get to Borken. I've got friends there.'

'Oh, well – maybe they'll speak for you,' said the boy. 'Look, my name's Pedro. What's yours?'

'Jack,' said Jack. He followed Pedro to a big motor caravan. Pedro rapped on the door, and a voice growled something from inside. They went in, and Jack saw a vast, enormously fat man sitting in a great chair. He had startlingly blue eyes, grey curly hair, and a beard that fell to his waist. He looked rather a terrifying kind of person.

'You speak for me, Pedro,' said Jack. 'I shan't be able to understand a word he says, unless he speaks English.'

'I spik the English,' said the old man, in his deep,

growling voice. 'English boys are good boys. Where you come from?'

'Well – nowhere particularly,' said Jack, wondering what to say. 'Er – I've just been wandering about since I came to this country. But I'm hoping to meet my friends at Borken.'

The old man fired a question or two at Pedro. Pedro turned to Jack. 'He wants to know if you've ever been in trouble with the police?' he asked. This was awkward. Had he been in trouble with the Hessian police? Well, no, not really, Jack considered. So he shook his head.

'He wants to know if you'll make yourself useful here?' said Pedro. 'He can see you must be used to circuses because you're carrying a talking parrot around with you. He says that if we stop here and there on the road to Borken, you can put your parrot on show if you like, and earn a bit of money by making it talk. He says, make it talk now.'

Jack rubbed Kiki's soft neck. 'Talk, Kiki,' he said. 'Make a noise!'

Kiki was always ready to talk. She raised her crest and began unexpectedly to sing at the top of her voice. 'Humpty-dumpty sat on a wall, Humpty-dumpty fell down the well, ding-dong-ding-dong, pussy's in the well, Fussy-Gussy, ha ha, ha! Wipe your feet and shut the door, oh, you naughty boy, pop-pop-POP!'

Kiki ended with a loud sneeze and a hiccup which sent Pedro into fits of laughter. Kiki cackled too, and then went off into her express train performance, which drew people from all over the field at once.

'Ha! She is goot, fery, fery goot!' said the old man, laughing, which made him appear as if an earthquake was shaking him. 'Yes – yes – you may come with us, boy.'

'I say! Your parrot's a wonder, isn't she?' said Pedro, as they walked back to his van. 'Would you like to sleep with me in my little van – look, the one behind Ma's? There'll be room for you if you don't mind a squash.'

Jack didn't mind at all! He would soon be on the way to Borken. Borken Castle! Would he find the others there? He'd get Bill over as soon as he could to rescue them – if only they were there!

16

With the circus

Jack liked Pedro very much. He was a born circus boy, with all their manners and ways, and he was sensitive enough to know that Jack did not want to talk about himself or what he was doing in Tauri-Hessia, wandering about with Kiki. So he asked him no questions, and Jack was very grateful.

He couldn't have told him the truth, and he didn't want to tell him lies! Perhaps when they were in Borken, and he knew Pedro better, he would be able to tell him a little – perhaps even get his help.

The circus went on the road that evening. The vans and lorries creaked out of the fields, and went clattering down the highway. It was a rough road, and the vans swayed about dangerously. Some of them had caged animals inside, and Jack watched them anxiously. What would happen if a van went over – would the animals escape? There were bears in one van, and two chimpanzees in another.

Kiki was a source of enormous amusement to everyone in the camp. Many of the circus folk could speak a broken English – enough to make themselves understood, anyway! They laughed at everything Kiki said. They brought her all kinds of titbits, and when they found that she was fond of tinned pineapple they raided the shops they passed, and bought tins of it!

Jack asked Pedro many questions. How far was Borken? Who owned the castle? Was it very old? Could anyone see over it?

Pedro laughed. 'Borken Castle – and the whole of Borken – and all the land we are passing through – is owned by the Count Paritolen. He lives at the castle, and as for letting anyone see over it – my word, they'd be clapped into a dungeon before they even got through the door!'

'He sounds rather fierce,' said Jack, gloomily. If the others had been taken to the Count's castle they wouldn't have a very nice time, with such a fierce captor!

'He's a very strong and determined fellow,' said Pedro. 'He hates the King, who is too strong for him. He'd like to make the young Prince Aloysius King – then he could rule the country himself, through the Prince, who would have to do as he was told.'

'I see,' said Jack, his heart sinking. What could he hope to do against a man like Count Paritolen?

'Is this Count the Prime Minister?' asked Jack, suddenly remembering what Gussy had said.

'No. His brother-in-law, Count Hartius, is Prime Minister,' said Pedro. 'They're both alike in hating the King – but Count Hartius is weak, where his brother-in-law is strong. It is his wife who rules him – a very clever woman, so they say – Madame Tatiosa.'

Jack listened to all this intently. He was beginning to have a clearer idea about things. How strange to be suddenly plunged into the middle of all this – to know the little Prince himself – to be so near the Castle of Borken, and to be on the land of Count Paritolen, who wanted to depose the King! It sounded like a tale in a book, a tale that had suddenly become real.

'How do you know all this, Pedro?' he asked.

'Oh, everyone in Tauri-Hessia knows it,' said Pedro. 'It may mean civil war, you see, and all the people fear that. If the King is deposed, and this young Prince is put in his place, the people will take sides and will be at one another's throats in no time – and circus people like us will have to get out of the country as quick as we can! So we keep our ears to the ground to find out what is going on.'

Jack was certain that he himself knew the latest news of all! He was sure that as yet no one in Tauri-Hessia knew that Prince Aloysius had been kidnapped from England, and was even now a prisoner in Borken Castle. But what was going to happen next? Would the plot take one step further, and news come out that the King had been killed – or put into prison?

Jack fell into deep thought – so deep that he didn't even hear Ma calling to him to come and eat. The boy suddenly felt that he had become a very important person in this plot – someone fortunately unknown to the plotters – but who might spoil the plot altogether if only he could manage to get into the castle.

'Penny for your thoughts!' said Pedro and gave him a punch. 'Wake up! You look very solemn. Anything on your mind?'

Jack shook himself, and smiled. Kiki had flown off his shoulder to Ma, who was fishing up some peculiar titbits for her from a big black pot.

'Polly put the kettle on,' said Kiki. She cocked her head on one side and looked at Ma. 'Bonnytageloota!'

Ma slapped her knees and laughed. She loved Kiki. She pointed to Kiki. 'She spik Hessian!' she called.

Jack was astonished. Now how in the world did Kiki manage to pick up the Hessian language? Really, she was a marvellous mimic. 'What does "Bonnytageloota" mean?' he asked.

'Top of the morning to you!' said Pedro, with a grin.

The circus stopped at a big village, and set up camp for two days. Jack was busy then. He had to give Pedro a hand in all kinds of ways – putting up tents, pulling vans into place, setting up the benches in rows, running here and there for the 'Boss', whose name Jack never could manage to pronounce.

The circus folk approved of Jack. He was willing and

quick, and he had good manners, which made him very popular with the women, who had got used to plain ways from the menfolk. Jack liked most of the circus people – they were kindly and generous, quick-tempered and cheerful – some were dirty and slovenly, too, not always very honest and sometimes lazy. They were good to Jack, and made him one of themselves at once.

They were a curious lot. There was Fank, with his three bears, one of the great draws of the show. The bears were all large, dark brown, and were natural clowns. They boxed, they knocked each other over, they lumbered round in a laughable dance, and they adored Fank, their trainer.

'Don't you go too near them, though,' Pedro warned him. 'They're treacherous. No one but Fank can manage them. Bad-tempered, bears are – have to be careful of them.'

The two chimpanzees were amusing fellows. They walked about hand in hand with their owner, a tiny woman called Madame Fifi. She wasn't much taller than they were! They really loved her.

Jack liked them very much, but soon found that they were dreadful pickpockets! They slipped their furry hands into his pockets without his knowing, and took his hand-kerchief, a notebook and two pencils.

Madame Fifi gave them back to him, with a laugh. She poured out something in French – or was it Spanish or Italian? She spoke so quickly that Jack couldn't even make out what language she was speaking. She saw that Jack didn't understand, and produced a few words of English.

'Bad boys!' said Madame Fifi, pointing a tiny finger at the chimpanzees, Feefo and Fum. 'Smack, smack, smack!'

There were Toni and Bingo the acrobats. Toni was a marvellous rope-walker, and raised a perfect storm of cheers and shouts when he performed on a wire rope high up in the big circus tent. He could do anything on it – run, jump, dance – even turn head over heels. Jack was always afraid he would fall.

'Why doesn't he have a safety net?' he asked Pedro. 'You know, he'd kill himself if he fell from that height!'

'Ask him!' said Pedro with a laugh. So Jack put the question to Toni, when the acrobat came across to talk to Pedro's mother. Toni was Spanish, but he understood English well, though he did not speak it fluently.

'Pah! Safftee net!' he said, in scorn. 'Onnly in Eengland is a safftee net put for me. I do not fall! I am Toni, the grrrrreat TONI!'

There was Tops, too, a clown whose great speciality was stilt-walking. It was absolutely amazing to see him stalk into the ring, as tall as a giant. He had big boots fitted on to the bottom of his stilts, and to most of the children in the audience he seemed a true giant, especially as he had a tremendous voice.

He had had a peculiar bicycle built for himself, very tall – and he could ride this when still on stilts. That brought the house down! Another thing that made everyone laugh till they cried was when someone in the ring wanted to talk to Tops. They brought in a long ladder and put it right up to his waist – then up the ladder somebody ran to talk to the clown at the top of it.

Tops was a funny little man in himself, always joking. His big voice didn't fit his small body. 'That's why he learnt stilt-walking,' Pedro told Jack. 'To be tall enough for his voice! That's what he always says, anyway.'

There was Hola, the sword-swallower. Jack watched him, shuddering. Hola could put a sword right down his throat up to the hilt! He would put back his head, and down would go the sword.

'I can understand his being able to swallow short daggers or knives,' said Jack. 'Well – not *swallow* them, exactly, but stick them right down his throat – but Pedro, HOW can he swallow that long, long sword of his? It's awful to see him. It makes me feel quite sick.'

Pedro laughed. 'I'll take you to Hola's van when he is in a good temper,' he said. 'He will show you how he does that.'

And one evening Jack had gone across to Hola's bright yellow van, and had been introduced to Hola himself, a tall, thin fellow with sad eyes. Pedro spoke to him in German, and Hola nodded and produced a small smile. He beckoned Jack into his van. In a big stand were all sizes of knives, daggers and swords. Jack pointed to a very long sword indeed.

Hola took it up. He put back his head, and down went

the sword, down, down, down his throat right up to the hilt. It wasn't possible! How could a man do that?

Up came the sword again, and Hola took it out of his mouth and smiled, still with his sad expression. He handed the sword to Jack.

And then the boy understood how Hola could do such an extraordinary thing. The sword was collapsible! It could be made to slide into itself, so that it became only the length of a long dagger. By a most ingenious mechanism, worked by a knob in the handle, Hola could make the sword shorter and shorter as he swallowed it.

Jack was most relieved. He was allowed to press the little secret knob, and see how the pointed end of the sword slid upwards into the main part, making itself into a curious dagger.

The circus folk were certainly interesting to live with! Jack couldn't help enjoying the strange, happy-go-lucky life, although he worried continually about Lucy-Ann and the others, and was impatient for the circus to go on to Borken. He was so afraid that he would be too late, if the circus was too long on the way.

'But I *must* stay with them,' he thought. 'It is the best possible hiding place for me. The police would certainly get me sooner or later if I wandered off on my own. But I WISH the circus would get on a bit faster. I simply *must* get to Borken soon, and do a bit of prowling round the castle on my own.'

17

Borken at last!

Kiki was a great success, not only with the circus folk, but with the people who came to visit it.

The Boss kept his word, and allowed Jack to show Kiki. Pedro helped him to make a little stand with a gilded perch set on a pole. Kiki was thrilled!

'I believe you think you're on a throne or something!' said Jack, grinning. 'Princess Kiki, the finest talking parrot in the world! Now – what about a song?'

Kiki was always ready to do anything if she could get claps and cheers and laughter. She really surpassed herself, and made Fank, the bear trainer, quite jealous because she drew such a lot of people to her little sideshow!

She sang lustily, and although she mixed up the rhymes and words she knew in a most ridiculous manner, the Tauri-Hessian folk didn't know that. They really thought she was singing a proper song.

Then she would always answer them if they said anything to her, though as they didn't speak English they had no idea what she was saying. Still – she answered at once, and usually went off into such a cackle of laughter afterwards that everyone roared too.

'Tikkopoolinwallyoo?' somebody would ask Kiki.

'Shut the door, fetch the doctor, Polly's got a cold!' Kiki would answer at once. Even Jack had to grin at her, she enjoyed it all so much.

Her noises were the biggest attraction of all. Her sneezes and coughs and her sudden hiccups made the village people hold their sides and laugh till the tears fell down their cheeks. They were rather overawed by her express-train-roaring-through-a-tunnel imitation, and they didn't understand the lawn mower noise because they did not use them; but they really loved the way she clucked like a hen, grunted like Fank's bears, and barked like a dog.

Yes – Kiki was a great success. Jack felt that she was getting very spoilt by all this fuss – but she did bring in money to him, so that he could pay Pedro's mother for the food she gave him, and for letting him share Pedro's little van.

The rest of the money he tied carefully up in his handkerchief, thinking that it might come in very useful if he needed any in Borken. He kept his hand on it when Feefo and Fum the chimpanzees were anywhere about. They would pick his pocket if they could – and he would lose all his savings!

'We shall be in Borken tomorrow,' Pedro told him, as

they got orders to pack up that evening. 'The Boss has got a pitch there – a good one too, at the bottom of the castle hill.'

Jack's heart leapt – ah, Borken at last. A whole week had already gone by, and he had been getting very worried indeed. Now perhaps he could get some news of the others. If only he could! Was Lucy-Ann all right? She would so hate being a prisoner in a castle.

They arrived in Borken the next evening. Jack first saw the castle from a long way off. It stood on a hill, and looked like something out of an old tale of King Arthur and his Knights. It was immensely strong, and had four sturdy towers, one at each corner.

'Borken Castle,' said Pedro, seeing it suddenly, as they came out of a thick wood, through which a rough road ran. He pointed to the great hill. 'In that castle many a prisoner has been held – and never heard of again. The dungeons are . . .'

'Don't,' said Jack, fearfully. 'Don't tell me things like that.'

Pedro looked at him in surprise. 'What's the matter? Not scared of a castle, are you?'

'No,' said Jack. 'Er – whereabouts were prisoners kept? In a tower? Anywhere special?'

'Don't know,' said Pedro. 'We might have a stroll round it sometime – but we wouldn't be allowed to go too near it, you know.'

The circus camp settled itself in a sloping field just at

the bottom of the castle hill. The townsfolk came streaming out to watch them set up camp. Evidently it was a great thing for them to have a travelling circus visiting Borken.

Children darted in and out, shouting and laughing. One small girl came running up to Pedro, calling out something excitedly. He swung her up into his arms, and she shrieked in delight, 'Pedro, Pedro, allapinotolyoota!'

Pedro replied in the same language. Then he turned to Jack, grinning with pleasure. 'My little cousin Hela,' he said. 'Her father married my aunt. He is a soldier in the Hessian army.' He turned and asked the excited Hela a few questions.

'Hela says her mother is with her father here – she is working as a maid in the castle for Madame Tatiosa, who is living at the castle now. And Hela lives in the castle too.'

This was news! Grand news! Now perhaps he would hear something about Lucy-Ann and the others. He stared at the small, lively Hela in excitement. But wait – wait – he mustn't give himself away. He mustn't blurt out questions without thinking. He frowned and tried to think what would be the best thing to ask.

'Pedro – has Madame Tatiosa any children?' he asked at last. 'Would she – er – would she like us to give a little show in the castle for them, do you think?'

'Madame Tatiosa has no children,' said Pedro. 'I can

142

tell you that. If she had, she would try to make one of them King! She is a clever, dangerous woman, that one.'

Hela wanted to know what Jack had asked. She listened and then went right up to Pedro and whispered something in his ear, her eyes dancing. Then she put her finger to her mouth as if telling him not to talk of what she had said.

'Silly child!' said Pedro. 'You have been dreaming!'

'What did she say?' said Jack, impatient to hear everything that Hela said. To think she lived in the castle. Why – she might see the others every single day!

'Hela says that Madame Tatiosa must have adopted some children, because sometimes, when she goes with her mother to one of the towers, she hears children's voices,' said Pedro, laughing. 'And she says that no one but Madame Tatiosa and Count Paritolen go right into that tower. She says it is very mysterious, but that no one must know, because when she told her mother what she had heard, her mother threatened her with a sound whipping for making up stories.'

'I see,' said Jack. 'Does she know which tower this is? Could she show us from where we stand now?'

'You don't want to believe a word she says, Jack!' said Pedro. 'She is a babbler, a story-teller, our little Hela!'

'Ask her, all the same,' said Jack, in such an insistent voice that Pedro did what he asked. Hela gazed up at the great stone castle. She pointed to the tower on the south side.

'That one,' she said, in a half-whisper to Pedro, and Jack understood, although she used Hessian words. She put her finger on her lips again to make sure that Jack and Pedro understood that they mustn't give her away.

Jack took her to buy some sweets. He wished intensely that he could speak the language of the country, but although he had picked up quite a few words – though apparently not so many as Kiki had! – it was impossible to hold any sensible kind of conversation with Hela. He didn't know enough of her language.

She chattered away to him and he didn't understand a word. He bought her the sweets and she flung her arms round him and hugged him. Then she ran off at top speed to show the sweets to her friends.

The camp was soon ready. The circus was to open the following evening. Jack had been very busy indeed, and was tired. But he was determined, quite determined that he was going to prowl round the foot of the great castle that night. Should he ask Pedro to go with him? No – it might be awkward to have Pedro there, if he *did* manage to get into touch with Philip and the others. He would have to explain everything to Pedro, and he didn't quite know how the circus boy would take his news.

Ma called out something to Pedro as he and Jack went to her van to get their evening meal. Pedro listened, and looked grave.

'What's up?' asked Jack.

'It's Fank, the bear-trainer,' said Pedro. 'He's feeling ill again. The Boss is very worried.'

'Why?' asked Jack. 'It will only mean that the bears don't perform, won't it? Anyway, Fank may be better by tomorrow.'

'It's a great loss to the circus when a big attraction like Fank's bears is taken off,' said Pedro. 'But there's worse to it than that. No one can manage those bears but Fank. They get quite out of hand when he's ill – won't let their cage be cleaned out – won't eat – fight one another. Once they even broke down their cage and got out. Fank had to crawl out of his bed in his caravan and somehow get them back. But it nearly killed him!'

'Poor Fank,' said Jack. 'Well, let's hope he is all right again by tomorrow. I don't particularly want great bears like that breaking down their cage and wandering about the camp, I must say. Fank's a wonder with them – I've watched him. He teases them and plays with them – and they fawn round him like dogs!'

'Not many people can manage animals as Fank can,' said Pedro. 'He had lions once – and two tigers – trained them all by himself. Then he suddenly said they didn't like performing and sold them to a Zoo. And yet they were the best trained lions and tigers in the world!'

'And now he's got bears,' said Jack. 'He must love animals very much, and they must love him. There *are* other people like that, Pedro. I know a boy who can do anything with animals, too.' He was thinking of Philip, of course.

'Ever tried his hand with lions, or tigers or bears?' asked Pedro. 'No? I thought not! I bet *they* wouldn't eat out of his hand. Cats and dogs and rats and mice and other creatures are easy to do what you like with – but not the big animals – the bears and the great cats!'

'No, I suppose not,' said Jack, thinking that Philip had never had the chance to work his magic on great creatures like those. 'Well – I hope Fank will be better tomorrow. *I* wouldn't like the job of cleaning out the bears' cage, I must say. I'd be afraid of their claws in my back the whole time!'

Jack did not go to sleep as quickly as he usually did, when he lay down on his mattress in Pedro's caravan. He didn't mean to. He was going to explore all round the foot of Borken Castle. He had bought a torch in the town that day. He didn't quite know what good he would do, wandering round in the dark – but it was the only thing he could think of. He had to do *some*thing!

He slid off the mattress as soon as he heard Pedro breathing deeply. He didn't want to wake him. He went out of the van, holding his clothes. He put them on in the darkness, and then, with the surprised Kiki on his shoulder, he set off to the castle hill.

If only he could speak to the others! If only he could make sure they were still all right!

18

Up to the castle!

Jack went stealthily out of the camp. All was quiet. There was no lamp or candle alight in any of the vans. The circus folk were tired out with setting up camp again, and had gone to bed early, in readiness for their grand opening the next day.

It was a starry night, with no moon, so there was not much light. It was not pitch dark, however, and Jack did not need to use his torch, once his eyes had got used to the darkness. The stars gave a faint light, just enough for him to avoid falling over anything.

He went up to the slope of the hill where the camp was placed. He came to a low castle wall. He shone his torch here and there, and found a place he thought he could climb, where the stones were rough and uneven.

His rubber shoes helped him a good deal. He wished he had rubber gloves on his hands, too, so that his fingers would not slip on the stones as he tried to grasp them!

He was over at last. He looked round cautiously, not

daring to put on his torch. He seemed to be in a small courtyard. He strained his eyes. He could make out the great bulk of the castle easily. It rose up high, towering about him, solid and strong. He despaired of ever getting inside – or even of getting in touch with Philip and the others!

He crept quietly over the courtyard, stumbling now and again over an uneven stone. He suddenly walked into something that scared him tremendously, and made Kiki give a frightened squawk.

Something wrapped itself round his head! What was it? In a panic Jack tore at it, and ran forward. But something flapped at him again, and covered his whole face. Desperately Jack switched his torch on and off for a moment, to see what was attacking him.

When he saw what it was, he gave a laugh of relief, and felt very silly. He had walked into a line of washing! A sheet had 'attacked' him, that was all – and the thing that had wrapped itself round his head was a jersey.

A jersey! Jack stopped. A jersey – such things were not worn in Tauri-Hessia. He stepped back and flashed his torch on again. Yes – it was either Lucy-Ann's or Dinah's. There was no doubt of it. So they definitely *were* there. Good, good, good! They were quite near him, somewhere. If only, only he could get to them.

He stood and considered. If the children were held in secret, then it was strange that their clothes should be washed and hung out on a line. People would see them and be surprised. Perhaps this courtyard was an enclosed space – a secret yard where nobody came, except possibly Madame Tatiosa. Would she wash the clothes though? She might, if she didn't want anyone to know about the children.

Perhaps Hela's mother was in the secret too? Perhaps *she* washed for the children, cooked their meals and so on? Somebody would have to do that.

There must be a way into the castle from this little yard – possibly a back way into the kitchen or wash-houses. Jack went towards the great walls of the castle and flashed his torch up and down. He would have to risk being seen by someone! He would never find out anything if he didn't use his torch now and again.

There was a small wash house there, as he had expected. He tried the door. It was locked. He shone his torch in at the window and saw coppers and pails and washing baskets. Yes, that was where the washing was done. What a pity the washerwoman had remembered to lock the door!

Jack looked at the little washhouse. It was built out from the castle wall. He flashed his torch to the roof of the wash house – and then higher up. He saw something that made his heart jump in excitement!

There was a window not far above the wash house roof – and as far as Jack could see it had no glass in it at all! It was a very old, narrow window and might never have had any glass, he thought.

'Now, let me think carefully!' he said to himself. 'If I could get up on the wash house roof – and then up to that window – I'd be inside the castle at once, and could look for the others. But how can I get up to the roof? I really don't think I can climb it, though it isn't very high.'

He couldn't. It was just *too* high for him to jump and catch hold of the guttering to pull himself up. There was no pipe he could climb up, either. Nothing at all.

'A ladder,' thought Jack, desperately. 'If only I could find a ladder.'

He began to hunt round, feeling rather hopeless. Kiki sat still on his shoulder, puzzled. She knew she must not make a sound, but she longed to, especially when a bat came swooping near her.

Jack went carefully round the yard. It wasn't very big. He came to a small shed. It was not locked, only latched. He opened the door carefully, horrified at the squeak it made, and flashed his torch inside.

Wonder of wonders! There was a ladder there! Jack could hardly believe his eyes. He went over to it. It was very old, and some of its rungs were missing – but it might do. It just might do! Anyway, he would try it.

He pulled it out of the shed, upsetting a can of some sort as he did so. The noise echoed round the yard, sounding extraordinarily loud. Jack halted, holding his breath. He quite expected to see lights flashing up in every window.

But none came. Everything was still and dark. He

heaved a sigh of relief. Perhaps nobody had heard the noise after all – or perhaps nobody slept on that side of the castle.

He carried the ladder over to the wash house. It was not very heavy, because it wasn't very long. Still, it would be long enough, he was sure.

He set it up against the wash house. It reached almost to the roof. He flashed his torch at the rungs to make sure which were missing. Then he put his torch into his pocket, and with Kiki flying round his head in excitement, he began to climb.

It certainly was a very old ladder! One of the rungs he trod on almost gave way. He hurriedly missed it and put his foot up to the next. He was very thankful when at last he was at the top.

Now to pull himself on to the roof. He managed to get there with a scraped knee and sat panting. Now for the next step – to get to the window above, in the castle wall itself.

The roof of the wash house was flattish, and Jack was able to make his way on all fours. He came to the wall. He stood up cautiously, feeling it with his hands, and then used his torch again.

'Blow! The window's just too high for me to pull myself up,' thought Jack, in deep disappointment. 'I can reach the sill with my hands – but can't get enough hold to pull up my body.'

He wondered if he could use the old ladder again. He

crawled back to it. He put his hand down and felt the top-most rung. Then he pulled hard. The ladder seemed a great deal heavier to pull up than it had been when he only carried it level. He tugged and tugged.

It was difficult to get it over the edge of the roof, but he managed it at last. He had to sit and hold the ladder by him for a while, because it had taken all his strength. He felt very pleased. Now he could put the ladder up to the window, and getting in would be child's play!

He managed to get the ladder to the castle wall, though it was a very dangerous business, and twice he nearly rolled off. But at last he was by the wall, and raised the ladder carefully. It was difficult to find a safe place to put it.

At last he thought he had got it as safe as he could manage. Now to go up. He hoped that the ladder wouldn't suddenly slip as he was climbing it. That wouldn't be at all a pleasant thing to happen!

He climbed up as quickly as he could, his heart thumping. Would the ladder hold? He got right to the top, and was just clambering on to the window sill when the ladder slipped beneath him.

It slid sideways, fell on to the roof with an appalling noise and then crashed down into the courtyard. NOW there would be people waking up and coming to see what the noise was!

Jack pulled himself right through the window. As he had thought, it had no glass, and probably never had had.

He jumped quietly down inside the window and crouched there, waiting.

He waited for three or four minutes, with Kiki nibbling his right ear, not making a sound. Then he stood up and stretched himself. He peered out of the window.

No – nobody was about. He could see no lantern or torch flashing, could hear no voices. This side of the castle *must* be uninhabited then, or surely someone would have heard such a tremendous noise!

Dare he flash his torch to see where he was? He waited another minute and then, hearing no sound, flicked his torch on quickly and off again. But he had seen enough in that second.

He was in a small room, piled with chairs and benches set neatly on top of one another – nothing else was there at all.

'Just a storeroom for extra furniture,' thought Jack. 'Come along, Kiki – we must remember we've got to find some other way of getting out of the castle – we can't get out the way we came in! That ladder is certainly out of our reach!'

He went to the door and looked out into what seemed a corridor. Not a sound was to be heard. It was pitch dark here, so he flashed his torch on again. Yes – a long stone passage without even a carpet runner on it. No pictures about. No chairs. This certainly must be a part of the castle where nobody slept.

He went down the long corridor, his rubber shoes

making no sound. He came to the end, where there was a window – a round one, with glass in it. He turned the corner and saw another long corridor, high-ceilinged, a little wider than the other, but still very bare.

Halfway down the corridor changed from bareness to comfort. A beautiful carpet ran down it, almost touching the walls each side. A big settee, covered in a golden damask, stood at one side. Great pictures hung on the walls.

'This is where I've got to be careful', thought Jack. 'There's even a lamp alight on that round table over there – a dim one, it's true – but still, enough for anyone to see me by!'

He went on. He passed an open door and looked cautiously inside. The light from another lamp just outside showed him what looked like a grand drawing-room. Tapestries hung all round the walls. Mirrors hung there too. A great carved table stood in the middle, its polished surface gleaming softly in the light of Jack's torch.

He went out into the passage again, and considered what to do. First – in which direction was the tower that Hela had said the children were in? He must go in that direction if he could puzzle it out. He would have to find stairs too and climb them.

He decided to go on down the corridor. He must come to stairs soon, leading up into a tower! He came to another door, wide open. He peeped inside. How grand this castle was! What magnificent furnishings it had!

The room must be a library. It had books from floor to ceiling. Goodness – had anyone ever read even a hundredth of them? Surely not!

A noise made Jack flick out his torch and stand absolutely still. It was a noise in the room he was standing in – the library. It came from behind him – a whirring, groaning noise. Kiki gave a small squawk. She was as startled as Jack. Whatever was it?

19

An adventure in the night

Whirrrrrr! Whirrrrrrrr!

'Ding-dong-ding-dong! Ding-dong-ding-dong! Ding-dong-ding-dong! Ding-dong-ding-dong! DONG, DONG, DONG, DONG, DONG, DONG, DONG, DONG, DONG, DONG, DONG, DONG!'

Jack sat down suddenly on a nearby chair, his heart thumping. It was only a clock chiming and striking! But what a start it gave him! Midnight – exactly midnight. Well – the people in the castle ought to be asleep, that was one thing to be glad of.

He got up and went back to the door. He went down the corridor again, and then, facing him round the next turning, he saw a great flight of stairs – a marble stairway, almost covered by a fine sweep of thick, beautifully patterned carpet.

'I suppose that leads down to the hall,' thought Jack. 'Down to the entrance. Well, that gives me a guide – let me see – if the front entrance is down there – then the

tower I want should be a bit further on. Come on, Kiki –
down the corridor again!'

And down the endless corridor went the two of them.
It was lighted by lamps, and was too bright for Jack's liking. The doors he passed now were shut. Perhaps they
were bedrooms. He certainly wasn't going to look in and
see!

He came to a sturdy oak door set in the inside wall. He
paused. The tower ought to be about here. Would that
door lead up to it? It looked different from the other
doors he had passed. He tried the handle gently. It was a
thick ring of iron and as he turned it sideways the door
opened.

Jack pushed it wide. Stone steps led upwards, lighted
by a dim lamp. He stood and debated with himself.
Should he risk it and go up? Yes – he felt sure this was the
way to the tower.

He tiptoed up and came to the top. He looked round
in surprise. He was on another floor now, and the layout
here was different from the one below. He was in what
looked like a great hall, draped with magnificent curtains.
A gallery overhung one end. There was a small platform
at the other end, and on it stood music stands. The floor
was highly polished, and Jack suddenly realized what the
hall was.

'It's a ballroom!' he thought. 'My word – what grand
dances they must hold here! But now I seem to have lost

my way to the tower again. Perhaps there's another stair somewhere!'

He went round the ballroom. On the other side, behind some curtains, he came to a door. He opened it and found that it led to a kind of ante-chamber. Opening off this was a stone staircase – a spiral stair that wound upwards.

'This is the tower staircase!' thought Jack, excited. 'It must be. Hallo – what's that?'

He could hear the sound of nailed boots on stone! Quick as lightning he slid behind a nearby curtain. The footsteps came nearer, stamped, turned and went back again. How extraordinary!

Jack put his head carefully round the curtain. Going down a stone passage opposite was a soldier, gun on shoulder. He must be on guard – guarding the tower! He disappeared down the passage, his footsteps sounding farther and farther away till Jack could hear them no longer. Then back he came again to the foot of the tower stairway.

Stamp-stamp! The sentry turned round once more and marched into the passage. Jack watched him again. He was dressed in Hessian uniform, very smart and decorative. Jack had seen many of these soldiers while he had been with the circus. Perhaps this soldier was Hela's father?

He waited till the sound of footsteps had completely died away again, then made a dart for the entrance to the spiral staircase. He ran up it swiftly, knowing that he had about half a minute before the return of the sentry.

Round and round wound the stairway, and at the top it grew so steep that Jack could no longer run up the steps, but had almost to climb!

He came to a little stone landing with a round window. A chest stood beneath the window, and an old chair stood beside it. Opposite Jack was a big, sturdy door, made of dark oak, and studded with great nails. He looked at it. Was Lucy-Ann behind that door? Dare he call her name?

He tiptoed to the door. He pushed. It was fast shut. He turned the great handle, but still it would not open. There was a keyhole there, but no key. He bent down to look through the keyhole, but could see nothing.

He could hear nothing either. Jack wished he knew what to do for the best. If he knocked on the door and called, he might find that the children were not there after all but that somebody else *was*. And the somebody might not be at all pleased to see him! Also, the sentry downstairs might hear him and come rushing up – and there was no way of escape up on this little landing!

And then he saw something in the light of his torch – something very surprising – something that told him for certain that the children *were* inside that room on the other side of the oak door!

A tiny creature had slipped under the wide space at

the bottom of the door, and sat there, looking up at Jack with large black eyes.

'Philip's dormouse!' whispered Jack, and knelt down slowly. 'Snoozy! You *are* Snoozy, aren't you! You're Philip's dormouse! Then Philip *is* in there!'

The dormouse was very tame. It had lived for some time with four children who adored it, petted it and had never once frightened it. Even Dinah had fallen under its spell, and loved it, though she would not let it run all about her as the others did.

And now here it was, on Jack's hand, its whiskers twitching, its big eyes watching him and Kiki. Kiki looked at it in surprise, but made no attempt to hurt it.

'Did you hear me, outside the door?' whispered Jack. 'Did you leave Philip and come to see who the midnight visitor was? How can I wake Philip? Tell me!'

An owl hooted somewhere outside the castle. The dormouse leapt from Jack's hand in fright and scuttled under the door. The hoot of the owl gave Jack an idea. The sentry would take no notice of an owl's hoot – but if he, Jack, gave a hoot just under the crack of the door, it would certainly wake up Philip. It would sound far away to the sentry, but very near to Philip! Far far better than banging on the door, which was a noise that might echo down the stairs and make the sentry come bounding up!

Jack lay down on his tummy. He put his face to the door, and placed his hands together to blow through his thumbs and hoot like an owl. This was the way to make a quavering hoot, so like an owl's that no one, not even an owl, could tell the difference!

'Hoooo! Hoo-hoo-hoo-hoo!' hooted Jack, and the noise went under the door and into the room beyond.

Jack listened. Something creaked – was it a bed? Then a voice spoke – and it was Philip's!

'Gussy! Did you hear that owl? It might have been in the room!'

But Gussy, apparently, was asleep, for he made no answer. Jack got up and put his mouth to the door, trembling in his excitement.

'Philip! Philip!'

There was an astonished exclamation. Then Philip's voice came, amazed. 'Who's that? Who's calling me?'

'It's me – Jack! Come to the door!'

There was a pattering of feet the other side and then an excited breathing at the keyhole.

'Jack! Good gracious! How did you get here? Jack, how wonderful!'

'No time to tell you my story,' whispered Jack. 'Are you all all right? How's Lucy-Ann?'

'We're all well and cheerful,' said Philip. 'We flew here . . .'

'I know,' said Jack. 'Go on – what happened?'

'And we were taken here by car,' said Philip, his mouth close to the keyhole. 'And Gussy was sick, of course. Madame Tatiosa, who met us in the car, was furious with him. She's here, in the castle – and her brother too,

Count Paritolen. We don't know what's happening, at all – have *you* heard? Gussy keeps worrying about his uncle.'

'His uncle is still safely on his throne as far as I know,' said Jack. 'But I expect they'll have a bust-up soon – everyone's expecting it. Then Gussy will find himself in the limelight!'

'Jack – can you rescue us, do you think?' asked Philip, hopefully. 'How did you get here? Gosh, I've been thinking you were miles away, at Quarry Cottage! And here you are, outside the door of our room. Pity it's locked!'

'Yes. If I only knew where the key was, it would be easy,' whispered Jack. 'Where does your window face? East or north?'

'North,' said Philip. 'It's just opposite a peculiar tower built all by itself – a bell-tower, with a bell in it. Gussy says it's an alarm-tower – the bell used to be rung when enemies were sighted in the old days. Our window is just opposite that. Now that we know you're here we'll keep looking out.'

'Give my love to Lucy-Ann,' said Jack. 'Is she in the same room as you?'

'No – the girls have another room,' said Philip. 'Look – let me go and wake them. They'd be so thrilled to speak to you.'

'All right,' said Jack, and then he stiffened. Footsteps! *Footsteps at the bottom of the spiral stairway.* 'Someone coming!' he whispered, hurriedly. 'Goodbye! I'll try and come again and we'll make plans.'

He stood up, and listened. Yes – that sentry was coming up the stairway. Had he heard anything? Jack looked round desperately. How could he possibly hide on this small landing? It was impossible.

The chest! He ran to it and flashed his torch on it. He lifted the lid. There was nothing inside except an old rug. He stepped inside the chest, Kiki fluttered in too, and Jack shut down the lid. Only just in time! A lantern flashed at the last turn of the stairs and the sentry came on to the landing. He held up the lantern and looked round. All was in order. He clumped downstairs again, his nailed boots making a great noise. Jack's heart slowed down and he heaved an enormous sigh. He got out of the chest and listened.

Philip's voice at the keyhole again made him jump. 'He's gone! He always comes up every hour. Jack – I never asked you. Have you got old Kiki?'

'Rather! She's been with me all the time,' said Jack, longing to tell Philip what a success Kiki was at the circus. But Philip didn't know about that either, of course. He didn't even know how Jack had got to Tauri-Hessia. What a lot there would be to tell him and the others!

Kiki began to whisper too. 'Blow your nose, shut the door, ding-dong-bell, Polly's got a cold. God save the King!'

Philip chuckled. 'It's good to hear her again. Shall I get the girls now?'

'No,' said Jack. 'I'd better go while it's safe. Goodbye, Philip.'

He went very quietly down the spiral stairway. He stood and listened. Where was the sentry? He must have gone down the passage again, on his regular beat. Jack slipped across the ante-room, and into the great ball-room.

He stood there for a moment, looking round the dimly lighted room. And then something caught his eye and he jumped.

On the far side was a great picture – and as Jack looked at it, it moved! It moved sideways across the wall, and behind it appeared a black hole.

Good gracious! Whatever was happening now?

20

The way out

A man's face suddenly appeared in the hole. Jack would not have been able to recognize it but for one thing – the man wore an eyeglass in one eye!

'The Count!' thought Jack. 'My word – what's he doing, popping up in secret places in the middle of the night?'

The man jumped down to the floor. A door at once opened near him and a woman came out. Jack recognized her, too. Madame Tatiosa, the pretty woman who had pretended to be ill at Quarry Cottage – the wife of the Prime Minister!

This was evidently a secret meeting between her and her brother. Where had he come from? Why was he so excited? The two of them spoke rapidly together and Madame Tatiosa seemed very pleased. She kissed her brother on both cheeks and patted him on the back.

'Her plans seem to be going well, whatever they are!' thought Jack. 'I bet it's something to do with the King.

They've probably arranged to capture him soon. That means that Gussy will be hauled out of that room and made to sit on the throne. I don't like the look of Count Paritolen. He's a nasty bit of work – and it's quite plain he's been up to something tonight!'

The brother and sister, still talking excitedly, went into the room from which Madame Tatiosa had appeared. The door shut. Jack heard the clink of glasses. They were going to celebrate something, perhaps? Things were obviously moving.

Jack wished fervently that Bill was there with him. But Bill probably didn't even guess that the five of them were in Tauri-Hessia. He had no means of knowing that they had come over by plane. He was probably hunting for them all over the place in England!

Jack looked at the hole in the wall. Where did it lead to? He felt impelled to go and look at it. He could still hear clinking and talking in the room nearby. He ran across to the hole, clambered on a chair and looked inside. He could see nothing, so he felt for his torch.

Then he saw the door of the room opening! There was only one thing to do – he must tumble inside that hole and hope for the best!

So in went Jack, almost falling over himself in his hurry. He found that there were steps there, and he slid down them, landing with a bump at the bottom. He sat there and listened, full of alarm.

But it seemed as if the Count and his sister hadn't

heard anything. He heard their voices in the distance. And then he heard something else! He heard a slight scraping noise, and the light that came into the hole where he was hiding was abruptly cut off.

'Gosh – the picture's gone back into place. I'm trapped!' said Jack, in alarm. He went up the steps and felt about at the back of the picture. The back was of stout wood, and fitted tightly over the hole. It wouldn't move even when he pushed it. He didn't like to do anything violent in case the Count heard him.

He put on his torch. He looked down the steps and saw a passage at the bottom. Well – it must lead to somewhere! It might even lead out of the castle! The only thing to do was to try it and see.

So Jack went down the steps again, and into a narrow little passage. He came to the conclusion that the passage must run just inside the walls of the room, at a little below the level of the floor. It went round at right angles quite suddenly – then there were more steps, very steep indeed.

Down them climbed Jack, thankful for his torch. It was very musty in the passage. He came to a place where there seemed to be a little light shining behind the left-hand wall. What was it?

Jack soon discovered! It was a small hole made in the wooden panelling there, and through it he could see into a dimly lit room – a room where people apparently met to discuss things, for there was a round table with chairs pulled up to it, and blotting pads and papers were set out neatly.

'Hm – a nice little spy hole,' thought Jack. 'Well – on we go. Wherever does this lead to, Kiki?'

Kiki didn't know – she only knew she was getting rather tired of this trip. She clung to Jack's shoulder and grumbled in his ear.

The passage went downwards again, not by steps this time, but in a steep slope. Jack found himself in a much narrower, lower passage now – he had to bend his head down. Two people would have found it difficult to pass one another. Kiki protested, because the ceiling kept brushing the top of her head.

'I wish I knew where this is all leading to, Kiki,' said Jack. 'I don't like it any more than you do! Hallo – here's a cellar, or something!'

The passage suddenly ended in a round cellar-like place, full of old junk. The entrance to this was only a round hole, through which Jack climbed, glad he wasn't as fat as the old 'Boss' of the circus.

'Now where do we go from here?' he thought. He flashed his torch all round. Nothing much to see but junk. Then he flashed his torch on the ceiling above his head – it was only about two inches higher than he was.

'A trap door! *Surely* that's a trap door! If only I can open it!' thought Jack.

He pushed hard – and it opened! It swung right back

and landed flat with a tremendous crash. It startled Jack horribly and made Kiki screech like a barn owl!

Nobody came rushing up. Nobody shouted 'Who's there?' Jack waited a minute and then clambered out. Where was he now? He began to feel he must be in a kind of nightmare, where nothing really led anywhere – only just on and on, steps, passages, holes, cellars, trapdoors – what next?

Again he shone his torch round. He was in a very tall, very narrow building of stone. Great ropes hung round him. He turned his torch upwards, and then he knew where he was!

'The bell tower! The tower that is just opposite Philip's room! That passage I've come down must be a secret way into the castle. Well – what a discovery!'

He went to the doorway of the bell tower. There was no door there, merely an archway. The place was apparently built just to hold the great bell and nothing else.

And then Jack discovered something that filled him with relief and joy. The bell tower was built *outside* the castle wall and not inside! He could run down the slope of the hill to the circus with nothing to prevent him – no walls to climb – no windows to jump from – there he was, outside the castle, walls and all.

'That's a bit of luck!' thought the boy. 'Come on, Kiki. We're out. Now we'll go back and get a bit of sleep!'

It wasn't long before Jack was creeping into Pedro's

caravan. The floor creaked loudly, but Pedro did not awake. Jack stripped off his things, thinking hard.

He felt pleased. Lucy-Ann and the others were safe. They had come to no harm. They were safe as long as Gussy wasn't King – then they might be held as hostages if the British Government sided with the present King, and demanded that he be put back on the throne. Jack could quite well imagine that Count Paritolen and Madame Tatiosa would delight in threatening all kinds of dreadful things where the children were concerned, if the British Government made things too uncomfortable for them.

'The thing to do is to rescue them quickly before Gussy's uncle is captured and Gussy's put on the throne,' thought Jack. 'I really must try and get in touch with Bill. But it will be difficult, because probably the people in this part of the country are on the side of the Count – and if I try to get news through to Bill, I'll be captured myself!'

He fell asleep thinking of it all. He had had a night of real adventure and he was tired out. He didn't even wake when Mr Fank's bears created a great disturbance in the early morning, and tried to break their cage down!

Pedro told him about it at breakfast time. 'Nobody dares to go near them,' he said. 'They haven't come to fighting each other yet, but they will. And then they won't be any use in the circus.'

'Isn't Mr Fank better then?' asked Jack.

'No. Worse,' said Pedro. 'The Boss is really worried.

Pity that friend of yours you told me about isn't anywhere near here. If he's as clever as you say, he might be able to quieten the bears and manage them!'

Pedro was joking, of course – but Jack sat up straight, and began considering the matter at once. He was sure that Philip *could* manage the bears, of course. Could he *possibly* tell Pedro where Philip was – and say that if Pedro would help him to rescue the children, Philip would try to do his best for the bears?

'What's the matter?' said Pedro, looking at him curiously. 'You seem excited about something.'

'Well – I *could* get hold of my friend, but only with help,' said Jack. 'He's – well, he's not really very far away.'

'Really? Why didn't you tell me?' said Pedro. 'Where is he?'

Jack hesitated. Could he trust Pedro? He asked him a question. 'Pedro – tell me truthfully – are you on anybody's side in this business about the King and the Prince Aloysius? I mean – what do you think about it?'

'Nothing,' said Pedro, promptly. 'I don't care which of them is King. Let them get on with it! The only thing I don't want is civil war here – we'd have to clear out of the country quickly then. Circuses and war don't go together! Why do you ask me that?'

'I might tell you later on,' said Jack, suddenly feeling that he had told Pedro too much. 'But I'll just say this – if I could get my friend here – with *his* friends too – we'd prevent civil war – Fank's bears would soon be under control and . . .'

'What rubbish you talk!' said Pedro, looking astonished. 'Stop pulling my leg. I don't believe a word of it.'

Jack said no more. But, as the day wore on, and Fank got no better, and the bears' behaviour got much worse, he felt inclined to tell Pedro a good deal more. It would be really marvellous if he could get Philip and the rest into the circus – what a wonderful hiding place for them all! Gussy would be too noticeable, of course. How could they disguise him?

'Of course! With that long hair of his and those thick eyelashes and big eyes, he could be dressed as a girl!' thought Jack. 'What a brainwave! I think I will tell Pedro everything. I'll tell him after the show tonight.'

The circus gave its first show at Borken that evening. It opened with the usual fanfare of trumpets and drums and the people of the town streamed up excitedly.

The bears, of course, were not on show, but otherwise everything went well. There was a good deal of grumbling from the townsfolk about the bears, because they had been well advertised, and some people demanded their money back.

'We must get those bears going somehow,' grumbled the Boss. 'We must pull Fank out of bed! We must get somebody else in. We must do this, we must do that! Where is Fank? Those bears will maul each other to death soon!'

After supper Jack spoke to Pedro. 'I want to tell you a lot of things,' he said. 'I want to get your help, Pedro. Will you listen? It is very important – very important indeed!'

'I am listening,' said Pedro, looking startled. 'Tell me all you want to. I will help you, Jack – I promise you that!'

21

A daring plan

'Where shall we go?' said Jack. 'In your van? Nobody can overhear us there, can they?'

They went inside the little van and shut the door. Pedro looked puzzled – what was all this about?

Jack began to tell him. He told him about Gussy staying with them at Quarry Cottage and how he turned out to be the Prince. Pedro's eyes almost fell out of his head at that! He told him of the kidnapping, and how he, Jack, had stowed away first at the back of the car, and then in the aeroplane, in order to follow the others.

'You're a wonder, you are!' said Pedro, staring at Jack in the greatest admiration. 'You're . . .'

Jack wouldn't let him say any more. He went on rapidly with his story, and brought it right up to date, telling Pedro of his adventure of the night before.

'I never heard anything like this in my life!' said Pedro, amazed. 'Why didn't you ask me to come with you? You knew I would. It was a dangerous thing you did, all by yourself.'

'Well – I'm used to adventures,' said Jack. 'I just had to find out about my sister, anyway – and the others too, of course. Now, Pedro – this is where I want your help. I MUST rescue the four of them before the King is kidnapped or killed, and Gussy is put on the throne. You see, if Gussy is missing, there wouldn't be much point in doing away with his uncle. They must have Gussy to put in his place, because they want a kid there, so that they can make him rule as they like. Count Paritolen and his sister, Madame Tatiosa, and the Prime Minister will be in power then. Do you understand?'

'Yes, I understand,' said Pedro. 'But I'm not used to seeing history happening before my eyes like this. I can't think it's real, somehow.'

'It is real,' said Jack, urgently. 'Very very real. And, Pedro, if we can get Philip here, in the circus, he could manage those bears as easily as Fank. I tell you, he's a wizard with animals – it doesn't matter what they are. Why, once, in an adventure we had, a crowd of Alsatian dogs chased us – we thought they were wolves, actually – and Philip turned them all into his friends as soon as they came up to him!'

Pedro listened to all this with a solemn face. He was much impressed. He had guessed, of course, that there was something unusual about Jack – but the story he had to tell was so extraordinary that he could hardly believe it all. He did believe it, though. He was sure that Jack would never lie about anything.

'Well – what do you want me to do?' he asked at last. 'I'll do anything, of course. But honestly, Jack, I don't see how we can rescue your four friends from the tower room of Borken Castle – locked in, with a sentry at the foot of the stairs! It's impossible!'

Jack sat and frowned. He was beginning to think it was impossible too. Plans had gone round and round in his head for hours – but none of them was any good.

He couldn't get in through that window over the wash house again, he was sure. The ladder would have been discovered by now, and taken away. Also – even if he did get in that way, how could he let Philip and the others out of that locked room? He didn't even know where the key was!

'And to go in the other way wouldn't be any good either,' he thought. 'Down that trap door and all through those passages – I'd only come up against the back of that big picture, and I've no idea how to make it move away from its place! And then again I'm no better off if I do – I still don't know where the key to that tower room is!'

Pedro sat and frowned too. To think that he and Jack could perhaps save the starting-up of a horrible civil war – and they couldn't think of even one sensible thing to do!

'Jack,' he said at last, 'do you mind if we tell someone else about this? My two best friends here are Toni and

Bingo, the acrobats – they might be able to think of some plan. It's their job to think of good ideas!'

Jack looked doubtful. 'Would they give my secrets away, though?' he said. 'It's important that nobody else should know what we know – once the Count suspected that anyone was trying to rescue the four prisoners he holds, he would spirit them away somewhere else, and probably hurry his plans on so that we couldn't possibly stop them.'

'You needn't worry about Toni and Bingo,' said Pedro. 'They're the best pals I ever had, and ready for anything. This is the kind of job they'd jump at – it's right up their street. I'll go and fetch them now.'

He went off across the field, and Jack sat and worried. He wasn't happy about telling anyone else. Soon the van door opened and in came Pedro with Toni and Bingo. They didn't look in the least like acrobats, in their ordinary clothes. They were slim, lithe young men, with shocks of hair and cheerful faces.

'What for you want us?' said Toni, the rope-walker, in broken English. 'It is trouble with the Boss?'

'No,' said Pedro. 'Look here, Jack – shall I tell them? – I can speak to them in Italian, which they know best, and it'll be quicker.'

'Right,' said Jack, wishing that he could use half a dozen languages as easily as this much-travelled circus boy.

He didn't understand a word of what followed. Pedro

spoke rapidly, using his hands excitedly just as all the Spaniards, French and Italian people did in the circus. Bingo and Toni listened, their eyes almost falling out of their heads. What a story!

Then they too began to chatter in excitement, and Jack could hardly contain himself in his impatience to find out what they were saying. Pedro turned to him at last, grinning broadly.

'I have told them everything,' he said. 'And it pleases them! They have an idea for rescue – a surprising idea, Jack – but a very very good one!'

'What?' asked Jack, thrilled. 'Not *too* impossible a one, I hope!'

'Shall I tell him?' said Pedro, turning to Toni, 'I can tell him more quickly than you.'

'Tell him,' said Toni, nodding his head.

'Well,' said Pedro, 'they got the idea when I told them how you escaped out of that trap door in the tall bell tower. I told them it was exactly opposite the window of the tower room – and they said it would be easy to throw a rope across from the top of the tower, to the window!'

'Yes – but I don't see what good that would be,' said Jack, puzzled. 'I mean – the others couldn't get across it – they'd fall.'

'Listen!' said Pedro. 'You have seen the trapeze swings that Toni and Bingo use in their acrobatic tricks, haven't you? Well, those swings can be attached to the wire rope by pulley wheels, and run to and fro. Would your friends agree to sit on a swing in turn, and be pulled across, hanging from the wire rope? It would be easy!'

'Good gracious!' said Jack, startled. 'My word! What an idea! It's not workable!'

'Si, si! It is wukkable!' said Toni, excitedly. 'We go up the bell tower. We get rope across to your friends – I walk across – easy! I pull swing behind me, hanging on rope. I place each boy or girl safe on swing – and I run back on rope dragging swing by wire – one, two, three, four times, and everyone is safe! Good idea, no?'

'Is it *really* possible?' said Jack. 'It sounds very dangerous.'

'Ah, no, no – it is simple, this way,' said Toni. 'I do it all, I, Toni!'

Bingo nodded his head. He apparently agreed with Toni that it was a good and perfectly possible idea. It would certainly only have been thought of by wire walkers or acrobats, Jack was sure.

'And then, zis boy – how you call him – Feelip – he will take Fank's bears and make them good?' said Toni. 'Everybody plizzed!'

'Everybody pleased,' agreed Jack, getting excited too. After all – these acrobats were used to things of this kind. It seemed nothing to them – though to ordinary people it appeared to be a very dangerous and quite impossible feat.

'Tonight we go,' said Toni. 'We have all things ready. We tell the Boss – no?'

'No – not yet,' said Pedro, considering. 'And not very much, when we do tell him. Nothing about the Prince or anything like that – only just that we've got a friend of Jack's to help with the bears. I'll have to think up some way of explaining the other three – but I'm not worrying about that yet.'

Toni and Bingo went off to their van, talking nineteen to the dozen. This was evidently something they were going to enjoy very much!

Jack could hardly keep still now. He kept on and on thinking about Toni's plan. Would it be all right? Would Lucy-Ann be too afraid to swing across on a trapeze-perch, and be caught at the other end of the rope by Bingo? What about Gussy? His hair would stand on end! And yet what better way was there? There wasn't any other way at all!

The circus opened as usual, and again there were grumbles about the non-appearance of the bears. Fank tried to get up, but it was no use. He couldn't even stand. The bears, hearing the circus beginning, and the shouts of the side-shows, became restless and excited. They had allowed no one in their cage that day, not even to clean it, and their food had been hurriedly poked between the bars.

They wouldn't even eat that! It lay in their cage untouched. They padded up and down the floor, heads down, grunting and growling all the time.

The show was over at last, and the townsfolk went

back to Borken, chattering and laughing. Jack helped Pedro to clear up the litter, pick up the fallen benches, and sweep the big circus ring.

'Thinking about tonight?' whispered Pedro as he passed him. 'I bet Toni and Bingo are! I saw Toni taking one of the trapeze swings out to shorten the rope, so that he could use it tonight.'

They had a late supper, and then Ma yawned. 'Bed!' she said, and creaked up into her caravan. The two boys went into theirs, and sat waiting for the acrobats to come and say they were ready.

There came a tap at the door. Pedro opened it. 'Come!' said Toni's voice, and Pedro and Jack slipped like shadows out of their van. The four of them made their way in the darkness up the slope of the hill. Above them towered the great castle, its shadowy bulk looking sinister and mysterious.

They came to the bell tower. Toni and Bingo had already had a good look at it in the daylight. 'In we go,' said Pedro, in a low voice. He flashed on his torch as soon as they were safely inside.

The torch lighted up the strong wire rope that Bingo carried, and the trapeze swing that Toni held. They all looked up into the roof of the bell tower. How were they to get up by the great bell?

'There are iron rungs up the wall,' said Toni. 'I go first! Follow me!'

22

Escape!

It was not difficult to climb up the iron rungs. Toni was soon up in the roof of the tower. Kiki was first though! She flew up from Jack's shoulder, and perched on the big bell, making a slight clanging noise that startled her considerably!

The iron ladder went right above the bell, which hung from a great beam. Above it was a stone platform, with an opening in it at one side for the iron ladder to pass through. Toni climbed up to the bell, and then through the opening above it, and passed on to the stone platform. Jack came next and then Pedro. Bingo was last.

There were arched openings like windows in the top of the tower opening off the stone platform, one arch facing each way – north, south, east and west. Toni peered out of the arch that faced the window in the castle opposite.

He considered the distance carefully. Jack peered out too. It seemed a long way to him in the darkness! He shivered. He didn't at all want to go on with this idea, now that he was up so high, and could see what a drop it was to the ground.

But Toni and Bingo treated it in a very casual, matter-of-fact manner. They talked to one another, and discussed it very thoroughly and with great interest. They apparently had no doubt at all but that they could do what they had planned.

Toni said something to Pedro, and he repeated it to Jack in English. 'Toni says he is ready. He says how can we attract the attention of your friends in the room opposite? They will have to help at the beginning.'

'If we flash a torch on and off – or perhaps hoot like an owl – Philip will come,' said Jack.

'We try the owl,' said Toni, and Jack put his cupped hands to his mouth and blew virogously between his two thumbs.

'Hooo! Hoo-hoo-hoo-hoo!' came quaveringly on the night air. Jack hooted again.

They waited, their eyes on the shadowy window opposite. Then, from the window, a light flashed on and off.

'Philip's there,' said Jack, joyfully, and flashed his own torch. 'Philip!' he called, in a low voice. 'Can you hear me?'

'Yes! Where are you? Not over there, surely!' said Philip, in an amazed voice.

'Tell him Toni is coming over on a rope,' said Pedro. 'But we've got to get the rope across first – so will he look out for a stone, tied on to a bit of string – and pull on it, so that the thicker rope can come across?'

'I know a better way than that!' said Jack, suddenly excited. 'Let Kiki take the rope across – not the thick heavy wire one, of course – but the first rope – the one that's fixed to the wire! She can take it in her beak.'

'Ah – that is good!' said Toni, understanding and approving at once. 'It will save time.'

'Philip – Kiki's coming across with a rope,' called Jack, cautiously. 'Look out for her. Take the rope and pull hard. It will bring across a wire rope. Can you find something to loop it to? It has a strong ring at the end – see that it is made fast.'

'Right. But how will . . . I say, I don't understand,' said Philip, bewildered.

'Call Kiki!' said Jack. Kiki had now been given the end of the rope in her beak. She was pulling at it with interest. 'Take it to Philip,' said Jack.

'Kiki!' called Philip. 'Kiki!'

Kiki flew straight across to him, carrying the end of the rope in her strong beak. She knew she had to take it to Philip, of course, but she had no idea that behind her came a whole length, paid out quickly by Toni!

She landed on Philip's shoulder, and let go the rope to nibble his ear. Philip just caught it in time. He wasted no time, but pulled on it hard. More and more rope came in – and then, joined to the ordinary rope, came the strong wire rope, heavy but flexible.

Philip hauled on that too until a tug warned him to stop. Now he had to fasten it securely to something. But what?

He had a lamp in his room and he lighted it, to see better. He kept it turned low, and held it up to see where he could fasten the ring that was on the end of the wire rope.

His bed had strong iron feet. Philip dragged the bed to the window, waking Gussy up with a jump as he did so, and then slipped the iron ring under one foot, pulling it up about twelve inches.

Now it should be held fast! The bed was by the window, the iron foot against the stone wall. Neither bed nor foot could move. The rope should be safe for anyone to use!

'What is it? What's happening?' said Gussy, sitting up in bed in surprise, unable to see much in the dim light of the lamp.

'Be quiet,' said Philip, who was now almost too excited to speak. 'Jack's out there. Go and wake the girls – but for goodness' sake *don't* make a noise!'

Over in the bell tower Toni pulled on his end of the wire rope. He pulled as hard as he could, and Bingo pulled with him. Was the other end quite fast – safe enough for Toni to walk across on it? He had to be quite certain of that before he tried to walk the rope.

'It's fast enough,' said Bingo, in his own language. 'It will hold you!'

Toni wasted no time. He got out of the stone archway, and stood upright on the narrow sill. Bingo held a torch to light up the wire stretching in front, from the bell tower to the window away opposite.

Toni tested the wire with his foot – and then Jack gasped in astonishment. Toni had run straight across the wire at top speed! There were his legs and feet, clearly lighted in the beam of the torch, running easily over the taut wire!

Toni reached the opposite window, and stood on the sill for a moment. Then he bent his head and climbed in, finding the bed just below the sill. Philip gripped hold of him, looking white.

'I say! What a thing to do! You might have fallen!'

The girls were now in the boys' room, having been awakened by Gussy. Kiki was with them, making a great fuss of them both. 'Who's this?' said Lucy-Ann, startled to see Toni jumping down to the bed. 'Philip – what's happening?'

'No time to talk yet,' said Philip, who wasn't really sure himself what was happening. 'We're being rescued, that's all!'

Toni was now busy pulling on a rope that he had brought across with him. He was hauling steadily on it – and along the wire, hanging neatly down from it, came a small trapeze swing – the one that Toni used each night when he swung high up in the circus tent, doing his tricks!

It clicked against the stone wall. Toni turned to Philip. 'You sit there,' he said, pointing to the swing below the rope. 'Sit still, see? And I will pull you over to Jack.'

Philip was startled. He looked at the trapeze swinging below the wire rope, running along it on a pulley wheel. So that was the idea! They were each in turn to sit on that peculiar swing, and be pulled across to the bell tower! Well!

'Hurry!' said Toni, impatiently. 'You first?'

'Yes,' said Philip, thinking perhaps that if the others saw him going across quite easily they wouldn't be afraid. He turned to Gussy and the startled girls.

'I'll go first and you watch me,' he said. 'Then Lucy-Ann – then you, Gussy – and you last, Dinah.'

He stood on the bed, and then swung himself up on the stone window sill. He held on to the rope outside, and suddenly felt Toni's strong hands under his armpits. It really wasn't very difficult to sit on the trapeze.

'I come!' said Toni, to the anxious watchers opposite, and he ran over the wire once more, pulling the trapeze back to the bell tower. Philip arrived there on the swing almost before he knew it! He was pulled off and dragged into the tower in safety. Jack found his hand and shook it hard. He found that he suddenly couldn't say a word! Neither could Philip.

Toni ran across again, pulling back the trapeze. Lucy-Ann was scared almost stiff with fright, but she was brave and managed to get on to the swing quite well, with

Toni's help. Away she went, giving a little gasp as she thought of the great distance to the ground below her.

Back came Toni with the swing, and Gussy was pushed forward to get on it. He was so frightened that Toni began to wonder whether he would fall off in the middle of his trip across the wire! But Gussy held on grimly, his teeth chattering – and almost burst into tears of relief when he got safely to the bell tower.

Dinah had no trouble. She wasn't afraid, and if she had been she wouldn't have shown it! She shot across easily, with Toni pulling her, as sure-footed as a cat.

Everyone suddenly felt very cheerful. Lucy-Ann hugged Jack without stopping. There was now such a crowd on the little stone platform at the top of the tower that poor Toni could hardly find room for himself!

'What about this wire rope?' said Pedro. 'How can we get it back?'

'We leave it,' said Toni. 'It is not possible to get it away. I have another.'

'Let's get down to the ground,' said Jack, half afraid that now things had gone so well, something might suddenly happen to make them go wrong. 'I'll go first.'

Soon they were all at the bottom of the tower. 'Silent, now,' whispered Jack, and they began to walk cautiously down the slope of the hill to the circus.

Lucy-Ann kept close to Jack, and he put his arm round her. He was very glad to know that his sister was safe. Gussy stumbled along, scared and puzzled. He didn't really seem to know quite what was happening!

'The girls can have our van,' said Pedro to Jack. 'You and I and Gussy can sleep beneath it.'

But before they could get to the van, a great clamour came on the air, and startled them so much that they all stood still in panic. Whatever was that tremendous noise?

'It's a bell – it's bells!' said Jack, putting his hands to his ears. 'The bell in the bell tower – and the bell in the church – and another bell somewhere else! Whatever's happening? Have they missed Gussy already?'

The circus folk all awoke and rushed out of their vans, marvelling at the pandemonium of noise made by the bells. Clang, clang, jangle, jangle, clang, clang! It went on all the time!

And then there came shouting from the town. Lights shone out, and still the bells went on and on. 'There are some ringing from the next village too,' said Jack, marvelling. 'It's to warn the people about something. What can it be? They *can't* know yet about Gussy escaping – why, except for Count Paritolen and his sister nobody knew Gussy was a prisoner.'

No – the bells were not ringing for Gussy. They were giving other news – serious news.

'The King! The King is gone! He has disappeared! He is nowhere to be found. The King is gone!'

The townsfolk shouted the news to one another in foreboding. What had happened to their King? Had he been killed? All the bells in the country rang out the news. Enemies had taken their King! Who? Why? Clang, clang, clang, jangle, jangle!

'My word!' said Jack, when he heard the news. 'We only JUST got Gussy out in time. Only just! Another half-hour and it would have been too late.'

'Yes,' said Philip. 'And I'd like to see Count Paritolen's face when he rushes to the tower room to get Gussy out of bed and put him on the throne – and Gussy's not there! The King gone – and no one to put in his place!'

Gussy howled. 'What's happened to my uncle?' he cried. 'Where is he? I don't want to be King!'

'Shut up!' said Jack, fiercely. 'Do you want every single person here to know you're the Prince? If someone gives you away, you'll be captured by the Count immediately! Go into that caravan and don't dare to make a sound!'

23

Beware the bears!

Jack hurried the girls and Gussy to Pedro's van. He hadn't reckoned on arriving back with them in the middle of a disturbance like this! All the circus folk were out of their vans; they were dressed in all kinds of shawls, coats and macs, hastily pulled over their night things, and were gathering together in frightened groups to talk.

It was just about the very worst time to bring Gussy to the camp. Suppose anyone recognized him? He would certainly have to be disguised at once.

Pedro realized this too. He knew, much better than Jack, what trouble the circus folk would get into if it was discovered that they were harbouring the Prince himself! They would all be clapped into prison at once. Pedro was very very worried.

'Jack! I'll have to tell Ma,' he said, desperately. 'I'll have to! She can hide Gussy better than anyone. Let me tell her. She'll help us.'

There was nothing for it but to say yes. Jack watched

Pedro go up to his mother and say something urgently. Then they disappeared up the steps of Ma's caravan, and shut the door. Jack looked at Philip, who was feeling bewildered at this sudden transition from confinement in the tower room to the excited turmoil of the circus camp.

The girls and Gussy were now safely in Pedro's own caravan – trying to peer out of the windows to see what was going on. Kiki had gone with them. Lucy-Ann almost wished she was back in the peace of the tower room! She couldn't understand exactly what was happening. Where was Jack? Why didn't he come and tell her?

Pedro came out of his mother's caravan and went straight over to Jack. 'It's all right,' he said. 'Ma's taken command! She's not a bit afraid of hiding the Prince – actually she rather enjoys something like this. She'll get him some girl's clothes, put a ribbon on that long hair of his, and keep him close to her. She says she'll tell everyone he's her little granddaughter, come to stay for a few days.'

Jack gave a chuckle at the thought of Gussy as a girl. 'He'll hate it,' he said. 'He'll kick up no end of a fuss.'

'Ma won't take any notice,' said Pedro, with a grin. 'She's quite likely to give him a few hard slaps, and my word, she's got a bony hand! I'll get him and take him to her. No one will recognize Prince Aloyisus when she's finished with him.'

Pedro went off, and Jack turned to Philip, who

grinned at him. 'Poor old Gussy! That's a wonderful idea though – Gussy will make a BEAUTIFUL girl!'

There came a sudden shouting from the other end of the camp – then screams. People began to stream away towards the two boys, shouting in fear.

'The bears! The bears! They're out!'

Toni came bounding up to Jack. 'Where's that friend of yours you said could manage animals? Oh, there he is. The bears are loose – they've broken three of the bars of their cage. See if your friend can help. Fank can't even get out of bed.'

Philip knew nothing about the bears, of course, and Jack hurriedly told him the details as they ran to the other end of the field. 'I hope you *can* do something with them, Philip. Toni helped me to rescue you on the chance that you *could* help. It will be a terrible loss to the circus if the bears get loose and have to be shot.'

One bear was still in the broken cage, afraid to go out because of the crowds. He was making a terrible noise. No one dared to go near. In a nearby cage Feefo and Fum, the two chimpanzees, were wailing in fright. Madame Fifi made sure they were safely locked in and ran over to Jack.

'Don't go near that bear, you two boys. He's dangerous. And look out for the others. They're loose.'

'Can't someone block up those broken bars?' said Philip. 'He'll be out soon.'

'Nobody dares,' said Toni. But little Madame Fifi dared! She ran to a brilliant flaring torch, stuck in a holder nearby, plucked it out and ran back to the cage. She thrust the pointed bottom end of the torch into the ground, just in front of the cage. The bear shrank back at the bright light and crouched down in a corner. He was afraid of the brilliance.

'That settles *him*,' said Philip, pleased. 'He won't attempt to come out while that light is there. Now – where are the others?'

'Over there – sniffing round the Boss's caravan,' said Jack, pointing to two dark shapes. 'I bet the Boss is shivering in his shoes inside the van!'

'Where can I get some meat?' panted Philip as they ran across the field towards the bears. 'Or better still, can I get honey anywhere – or treacle?'

'Treacle! Yes, Ma's got a whole jar of it,' said Jack, remembering. 'I'll get it.'

He raced off to Ma's caravan, burst in and demanded the treacle. Gussy was there, standing in silken vest and pants, protesting loudly. Ma was evidently getting to work on him! She didn't seem to be at all surprised at Jack bursting in to ask for treacle.

'On the shelf,' she said, and went on brushing out Gussy's hair.

Jack found the big stone jar and fled back to Philip with it. Philip had now gone close to the bears, who turned to look at him suspiciously.

'They've already injured one man,' said Jack, in a low voice. 'Look out, won't you, Philip?'

'I'll be all right,' said Philip. 'Keep out of sight, Jack.' He took the jar of treacle, dipped his hands in it and smeared them up to the wrists with the thick, sweet syrup.

Then he walked towards the bears, pouring a little of the syrup out on the grass as he went. The bears growled warningly. Philip turned and went back again. He sat down with the jar of treacle and waited.

By now many people were watching. Who was this boy? What was he doing, meddling with two dangerous bears? They watched in fearful curiosity, ready to run at any moment.

Jack stood out of sight – but near enough to run to Philip's help if necessary! He didn't think it *would* be necessary; he had absolute faith in Philip's ability to manage any animal.

The bears soon smelt the syrup that Philip had spilt here and there on the grass. They loved the sweetness of treacle. Fank sometimes gave it to them for a treat – and there was nothing they liked better than to have an empty syrup tin given to them, and to be allowed to lick it, and put their great paws inside.

They sniffed, and went towards the first spots of treacle on the ground. One bear found them and licked eagerly. The second bear growled at him and tried to push him aside – but suddenly smelt another few spots of treacle further on! He lumbered on clumsily and licked eagerly.

As soon as the bears realized that there was treacle about, they began to grunt excitedly. They had refused food for two days now, and they were hungry. They sniffed eagerly for more treacle.

The watching people held their breath as they saw the two great clumsy creatures getting nearer and nearer to the boy sitting on the ground. Surely he was in danger?

'Who is he? He ought to be warned!' they said. But Toni and Bingo hushed them.

'Be quiet! He is Jack's friend, a wonder with animals! Give him a chance! He can run if the bears threaten him!'

The first bear was now quite near Philip, his head close to the ground as he sniffed about for more treacle. Philip put his hand into the jar he held, and took it out, waving it slowly in the air so that the bear could get the full scent of it.

The bear raised his head and saw Philip. He backed away a little and gave an angry grunt. Who was that sitting on the ground? His eyes gleamed an angry red in the light from a nearby lamp. A little sigh of fear went through the anxious crowd.

And then Philip spoke. He spoke in what Jack called his 'special' voice – the voice he always kept for animals. It was a low, monotonous voice, a gentle, kindly voice, but somehow it was a voice that had to be listened to. 'A sort of hypnotizing voice,' thought Jack, as he stood watching.

The bear listened. He grunted again, and backed

away, bumping into the second bear. But still Philip's voice went on. What was he saying? Jack couldn't hear. How did he know how to talk to animals like this? And why did they all listen? The watching circus folk knew that most animal trainers used a special tone of voice when they petted their animals – but here was a strange boy talking to frightened and suspicious bears – and yet they listened.

The second bear came a little nearer, his ears pricked. He sniffed. He sniffed not only the treacle, but Philip's own particular smell. He liked it. It was a friendly smell. The bears always sorted out people into two kinds – those whose smell they liked and those they didn't.

He lumbered right up to Philip and sniffed at him, ready to strike if the boy moved. A little scream came from someone in the crowd, but the bear took no notice.

Philip went on talking, and now his voice was so honeyed and persuasive that even the crowd began to feel his spell. The bear licked Philip's hand, which was covered in treacle. Philip did not move. The bear went on licking, quite unafraid.

The other bear came up, and, seeing how unafraid his brother was, he took a quick lick at Philip's other hand. In two or three seconds both bears were grunting in delight at so much treacle. This boy was a friend! They didn't know who he was, but they were quite sure he was a friend.

Philip talked all the time, monotonously and kindly.

He thought he could now dare to move, so he lifted one hand slowly, put it into the jar beside him, and then took it out covered with treacle again.

One bear lay down beside him to lick in comfort. Another sigh at once went through the tense crowd. Philip gave the jar to the other bear, and then with his free hand began to fondle the bear lying beside him. It grunted in pleasure.

Now the bears were happy and at peace. They had found someone they liked and trusted. Philip knew that he had them under control – if only the crowd didn't do something silly – make a sudden noise, or come surging towards him. But the circus folk knew better than that. They were used to animals.

Philip stood up, doing nothing quickly – all his movements were smooth and slow. He picked up the jar, and with his other hand on one bear's neck, began to walk to the cage. The bears followed, shambling along quietly, licking their lips.

Philip took them right to the cage, undid the door and let them shuffle in. He put the treacle jar inside, shut the door, and went quietly outside.

And then how the people cheered! 'He's a wonder! Who is he? Tell Fank the bears are safe. Who *is* this boy?'

24

Morning comes!

Philip called to Jack. 'Jack – see if you can get some meat – plenty of it – and bring it to me.'

'*I'll* get some,' said Toni, and raced off. He came back with a basket containing great slabs of horse meat. Philip took it. He opened the cage door and threw in the meat, talking cheerfully to the hungry bears.

Now they were ready for their meal. They were no longer sulky, scared or angry. They were just three very hungry bears, and they fell on the meat and gulped it down.

'Let them have as much as they will eat,' said Philip. 'Then they will go to sleep. While they are asleep, someone must mend their cage bars. Keep that light in front now – none of them will venture out of the broken bars while that light is there.'

Everyone gathered round Philip. 'He's a friend of Jack,' they said to one another. 'He fetched him here because he is good with bears. He must have come from another circus. Look – the Boss wants him.'

The Boss had watched everything from his caravan window. He was most impressed and extremely thankful. Pedro told Philip that the Boss had sent for him, and he and Jack and Philip went up the steps of the Boss's big caravan.

The Boss poured out praise and thanks in a mixture of several languages. Pedro interpreted with a grin. 'He says, what can he do for you? He says you've saved the bears from being shot. He says, ask anything you like and you can have it, if he can give it to you!'

Jack answered quickly. 'There's only one thing we want. Now that there is this upset in Borken, can we all stay with the circus? Philip will be glad to look after the bears, as long as Fank is ill – but he has girls with him, our sisters – can they stay too? We don't like to let them go off by themselves, in case civil war starts up in Tauri-Hessia.'

Pedro interpreted. The Boss quite thought that these 'sisters' were circus performers too. He nodded his head. 'Yes – you may let them stay. If they have tricks or shows of their own, they may get a chance here. But we must strike camp tomorrow – it will be dangerous to stay here in Borken any longer. The Count Paritolen owns this land, and as it is probably he who has something to do with the King's disappearance, it would be best for us to leave before trouble starts.'

'What does he say?' asked Jack, anxiously. Pedro translated all this into English, and the two boys were much relieved. Good! They could all stay with the circus, and would leave almost immediately with the circus folk! They would soon be out of the danger zone – and then perhaps they could get a message to Bill.

The boys went down the steps of the van with Pedro. They made their way to Pedro's own little van, feeling that they simply must have a good long talk. It was about two o'clock in the morning now, but none of the three boys felt tired – they were far too strung up with the happenings of the night.

The circus folk as they passed clapped Philip on the back. He smiled and nodded, and then at last all three were in the little van with the two girls and Kiki.

'Shut the door,' said Kiki at once. 'Wipe your feet. Fetch the King!'

'I wish we could, Kiki,' said Jack, with a laugh, as the parrot flew on to his shoulder. 'But don't you start talking about the King. Oh – Lucy-Ann – you nearly had me over! What a hug! It reminds me of the bears!'

'I can't help it!' said Lucy-Ann, and gave Philip a hug too. 'I was so anxious about you and Philip, with those bears. It all seems like a horrid dream. I was longing for you to come back to us. Gussy's gone too. Is he really going to be a girl?'

'He is,' said Jack, sitting down on the mattress. 'Now, we've got to talk and make plans. First of all, because of

Philip's grand performance with the bears, the Boss has said that we can all stay with the circus. We couldn't have a better hiding place!'

'That's true,' said Dinah. 'But suppose the Count makes a search for us – and his men are sent here to look, among other places. Gussy might not be recognized if he's dressed up as a girl – but what about me and Lucy-Ann and Philip? We're all dressed in the English way – we'd soon be noticed.'

'Yes. I hadn't thought of that,' said Jack. 'I'm too English, as well. Pedro – I've got some money saved up that I made out of Kiki's performances – could you buy some Hessian clothes for us early today?'

'Ma will fix you all up,' said Pedro. 'She's a wonder with her needle! She'll get some cloth from old Lucia, the woman who's in charge of the circus clothes. And we'll borrow some grease paint from Toni and give you all tanned Tauri-Hessian faces! But don't go speaking English!'

'No, we won't. We'll talk a wonderful gibberish of our own!' said Philip, with a laugh. 'We'll come from Jabberwocky, and talk the Jabberwock language! It goes like this – Goonalillypondicherrytapularkawoonatee!'

Everyone laughed. 'Good!' said Pedro. 'I'll tell any searchers that you are Jabberwockians, and then you can talk like that if they ask you anything. By the way, where *is* Jabberwocky?'

Kiki suddenly launched with delight into the

Jabberwockian language. They all listened to her and roared. 'You're a very fine specimen of a Jabberwockian parrot!' said Jack, stroking her. 'Go to the top of the class!'

Dinah gave an enormous yawn, at once copied by Kiki. It made everyone begin to feel terribly sleepy. 'Come on – we'll be striking camp fairly early,' said Pedro, getting up. 'Sleep in peace, girls. We three boys will be just under the van, on a couple of rugs. As for Gussy, I expect he's snoring in Ma's extra bunk, looking like a beautiful little girl!'

Gussy was not asleep, however. He lay in the small bunk, listening to Ma's deep breathing and sudden snorts. He was very angry and very humiliated. Ma had seen to him properly! She had tried his hair this way and that, and had finally decided that he looked more like a girl with a small bow at each side rather than with one big one on top.

She had also looked out some clothes – a longish skirt, rather large, very highly coloured, and decidedly ragged – and a small red blouse with a green scarf tied skittishly round the waist. Gussy could have cried with shame.

It wasn't the slightest bit of good arguing with Ma. In fact, when Gussy refused to stand still while his bows were being tied, Ma had given him a hefty slap on a very tender place, which had given Gussy such a tremendous shock that he couldn't even yell.

'You know I'm a Prince, don't you?' he said, fiercely, under his breath.

'Pah!' said Ma. 'You're just a boy. I've no time for Princes.' And she hadn't.

Now Gussy was trying to go to sleep, his hair still tied with bows, and a peculiar sort of garment on him that looked half like a night gown and half like a long coat. He went over the exciting escape in his mind, and shuddered. No – he wouldn't think about that awful rope and the trapeze swing. He wondered about his uncle and shuddered again. Was he killed? Poor Gussy's thoughts were not pleasant ones at all.

The morning came all too soon for the five tired children. Philip went across at once to the bears' cage to see how they were. The bars had been mended and strengthened. The bears, looking extremely well fed, were half asleep – but as soon as they saw Philip they padded to the bars and grunted amiably. One bear tried to reach him with his paw.

'Good – they're quite all right,' said Philip, and gave them a little talk to which they listened entranced, as if they understood every word!

Fank was better – but still could not stand up. Philip went to see him, and the little man took his hand and poured out a stream of completely unintelligible words. Philip knew what he was saying, though! Here was a grateful man if ever there was one! Fank loved his bears as if they were his brothers, and he had been almost mad with anxiety the night before, when he heard they had escaped.

'I'll take them on till you're well,' said Philip, and Fank understood, and shook Philip's hand fervently.

The next thing was clothes. The camp was to set off in three hours, so Ma had got to hurry if she was going to get the four of them clothes that would disguise the fact that they were English.

She went to Lucia, an old bent woman who kept the clothes of the circus folk in order – not the ordinary ones they wore every day, but their fine ones, worn in the ring – their glittering capes and skirts, their silken shirts and magnificent cloaks. These were valuable, and old Lucia's needle was always busy. So was her iron. Nobody could press fine clothes as well or as carefully as Lucia.

By the time the circus folk were ready to strike camp, nobody would have recognized Dinah, Lucy-Ann, Philip and Jack! Toni had lent them grease paint and each of them was tanned and looked like a Tauri-Hessian – face, neck, legs, and hands! The girls wore the Tauri-Hessian dress – long skirts and shawls, and bright ribbons in their hair.

The boys looked just like normally brought up boys of the country, and seemed to have grown older all of a sudden. Lucy-Ann stared at Jack in surprise, hardly recognizing this brown youth, whose teeth gleamed suddenly white in his tanned face.

Ma was pleased with her efforts, but most of all she

was delighted with Gussy. Nobody, *nobody* could possibly think that Gussy was anything but a girl. He looked really pretty! All five of them, Pedro too, roared with laughter when poor Gussy came down Ma's caravan steps, looking very red in the face, very angry, and very ashamed.

'Dis is my little grandchild, Anna-Maria!' said Ma, with a broad smile. 'Be kind to her, plizz!'

Gussy looked as if he was about to burst into tears. 'Yes, go on, cry!' said Philip, teasing him. 'That'll show people you aren't Anna-Maria!'

Dinah gave him a punch. 'Some girls do cry!' she said. 'Oh dear – doesn't Gussy – I mean Anna-Maria – look priceless?'

'Smashing!' said Jack. 'Honestly, he's as pretty as a picture. Thank goodness for his long hair – that's what helps him look like a girl more than anything!'

'I cut it short soon, soon, *soon*,' said poor Gussy, furiously. 'Snip-snip – like that!'

'You can't. You told us that Princes of this country have to wear it long, like you do,' said Dinah.

'I will *not* be a Prince then,' said Gussy. He looked suddenly very forlorn, and gazed at Lucy-Ann beseechingly, feeling that she had the kindest heart of the lot.

'Do not tizz me,' he begged. 'I hate zis. I am full of shamefulness.'

'All right, Gussy, er – Anna-Maria,' said Jack. 'We won't tizz you. Cheer up – you'll be a Prince again before long, I'm sure.'

'If my uncle is alive, I will be,' said Gussy, soberly. 'If he is dead – I must be King!'

'God save the King,' said Kiki, devoutly, and raised her crest impressively. 'Fetch the doctor and save the King!'

25

The camp is searched

Soon a long procession of vans was going down the winding road that led away from Borken. The two girls and Gussy were in Pedro's little van, and he was driving the small skewbald horse that belonged to him.

Jack was driving Ma's van for her, and the old lady looked really happy. She loved a bit of excitement, and she roared with laughter whenever she caught sight of poor Gussy.

Philip, of course, was driving the van in which the bears' cage was built. Toni was driving Fank's little living-van, whistling cheerfully. Fank lay on his mattress inside, glad to feel better, and to know that 'that wonder boy' Philip had got his bears in charge. He felt full of gratitude to Philip – and to Toni too for so cheerfully driving his van for him. The circus folk were always ready to help one another. That was one of the nicest things about them.

The vans rumbled along the road, going very slowly,

for neither the bears nor the chimpanzees liked going fast. They were all excited at being on the move again. Feefo and Fum chattered away together, looking through the window of their van.

'Where are we going?' Dinah asked Pedro, through the open window of the van. Pedro shrugged his shoulders. He had no idea.

'We must get away from Borken, where a lot of trouble may start,' he said, 'and try to find somewhere more peaceful. We shall probably make for some country road, and keep away from all the main roads. Soldiers will use those, if trouble starts.'

Dinah went back into the van. The Tauri-Hessian dress suited her well, and she looked exactly right in it. 'We're making for some country road,' she told Lucy-Ann. 'It's a pity we still can't get in touch with Mother or Bill. They really will be dreadfully worried about us by now.'

'I suppose the police will have been told and will be hunting everywhere for us – but in England instead of here!' said Lucy-Ann. 'Well, anyway, we're safe for the moment, and out of that tower room. I was getting tired of that! Nothing to do all day but to play games with those funny cards they brought us!'

They all stopped for a meal at about one o'clock. The vans stood at one side of the road, and the circus folk sat beside them and ate. It was like summer, although it was only April. The sun was very hot, and masses of brilliant flowers were out everywhere.

Philip's little dormouse came out to share the meal with him. He had had it with him all the time. It was scared by the noisy talk of the circus folk, and only appeared when things were quiet. It sat on the palm of Philip's hand, enjoying a nut, its big black eyes now and again glancing up at the boy.

'I don't know what we'd have done without you, Snoozy, when we were shut up in that tower room,' said Philip, softly. 'You kept us all amused with your little games and antics, didn't you? And you told Jack where we were, the other night – you ran under the door to him!'

Soon they were on the way again. The bears settled down to sleep, happy to know that Philip was driving them. He had fed them himself again when the procession halted for a meal, and the bears grunted at him happily. Fank heard them and was happy too.

The procession wound down the road, came out into a main road, and went down that, intending to turn off at a country road about two miles on. But halfway down something happened.

Three powerful military cars swept by the procession, and drove right up to the head of it. Then they stopped, and soldiers leapt down from the cars, with a captain in command.

'Halt!' he said to the front driver, and the whole procession came to a stop. The circus folk looked worried.

What was this? Soldiers already? And why were *they* being halted? They had done nothing wrong!

They jumped down from their vans, and gathered together in little knots, waiting. Jack poked his head back into Ma's van, which he was driving. 'This is it, Ma,' he said. 'I think the vans are going to be searched. Give Gussy something to do, and scold him as if he was your grandchild. Gussy, you're a girl, remember – so don't answer back, or even say a word, when the men come along. Look shy if you can.'

Pedro also knew what was about to happen. He called to the two girls, 'Come out, and mix with the circus folk. Go with Toni and Bingo. I'll come too. I'll put my arms round you both as if you were my sisters or my friends.'

Philip, however, didn't move. He decided that he was in a very good place, driving the bears' van! The men would be sure to upset the bears and he would have to pacify them. He would appear to the men to be a bear trainer!

The captain found the Boss. Pedro heard him talking to him in sharp tones.

'We are going to search your vans. We suspect you have someone here we want. It will be the worse for you, if you have. I warn you to give him up now, at once, because when we find him you will be severely punished.'

The Boss looked surprised. He was sitting in his great chair inside his van. 'I do not know what you mean,' he said. 'Search my vans! You are welcome!'

The Boss thought that the soldiers were looking for a deserter, a young man, perhaps. He did not know they were hunting for a small boy, and certainly had no idea they were after the little Prince Aloysius!

The captain gave a sharp command. His soldiers marched down the sides of the vans, keeping a watch for anyone who might try to hide in the wayside bushes. Then they began to search carefully, probing each van, lifting up piles of rugs or clothes to see if anyone could be hidden there.

They stopped at the sight of Philip. They had been told that although they must at all costs find Gussy, there were three other children, too, to look for. Children whose presence in the camp would tell them the Prince was somewhere about too.

They came up to the bears' van, their heels clicking sharply. Their loud voices angered the three bears, and they growled and flung themselves at the bars.

Toni came up and spoke to them, telling them to keep out of sight of the bears.

'We had trouble with them yesterday,' he said, 'and this boy, who helps the trainer, only just managed to keep them under control. As you see, the bars of the cage were broken and had to be mended. Keep out of sight, please, or they will break the bars again.'

Philip didn't understand what Toni was saying, but guessed. He decided that the best thing he could do to avoid being questioned was to get inside the bears' cage, and pretend to quieten them. So in he went, and the bears fawned round him in delight.

The soldiers watched from a safe distance. The captain was satisfied. Obviously this boy belonged to the circus, and travelled as a helper with the bears. He could not be one of the boys they had been told to look out for. They went on to the next van, and Toni winked at Philip.

'Good!' he said. 'Keep there. You are safer with the bears than anywhere else!'

The soldiers went from van to van. They hardly glanced at Dinah or Lucy-Ann, who, with Pedro's arms round them, were standing watching the two chimpanzees. Madame Fifi had taken the opportunity of giving them a little airing.

The captain, however, glanced sharply at Pedro. Could he be one of the boys they sought? He beckoned to him. Pedro came over, still with the girls, smiling, and at ease.

The captain snapped something at him in Tauri-Hessian. Pedro answered smoothly, pointing to his mother's van. He was saying that he travelled with his mother, and his little cousin, Anna-Maria.

'And these two girls?' said the captain, sharply.

'They are with the circus too,' said Pedro. 'They belong to the boy who manages the bears – you have seen him. They are Jabberwockians, and speak very little Hessian. But they speak French if you would like to ask them anything.'

Dinah heard Pedro say the word 'Jabberwockians' and

guessed that he was saying that she and Lucy-Ann belonged to Jabberwocky! Dinah immediately poured out a string of utter gibberish to the captain, waving her hands about, and smiling broadly. Lucy nodded her head now and again as if she agreed with her sister!

'All right, all right,' said the captain, in his own language. 'It's all nonsense to me, this. I can't understand a word! What is she saying?'

Pedro grinned. He told the captain that Dinah thought him very magnificent, much grander than captains in Jabberwocky. He was pleased. He saluted the two smiling girls smartly, and went away, satisfied that they were certainly not English. He really must find out where the Land of Jabberwocky was – he didn't seem to have heard of it. These circus folk came from queer places!

And now the soldiers had reached Ma's caravan. Jack was still sitting in the driver's seat, Kiki on his shoulder. He had warned her not to talk, because he was afraid her English words might give them away. 'But you can make noises,' he told her, and Kiki understood perfectly.

She raised her crest as the men came near and coughed loudly. The soldiers looked at her in surprise.

'Powke,' said Jack, patting Kiki. 'Powke, arka powke.' He knew that this meant 'Clever parrot,' because the people who had come to marvel at Kiki when she had been on show, had so often said those two words. 'Arka powke!' Clever parrot!

Kiki gave a loud hiccup, and then another. The soldiers were tickled, and roared with laughter. Then Kiki clucked like a hen laying eggs, and that amused them even more.

This was the kind of thing Kiki liked. It gave her a wonderful opportunity for showing off. She put down her head, looked wickedly at the soldiers, and gave them the full benefit of her aeroplane-in-trouble noise.

They were extremely startled, and stepped back at once. Kiki cackled idiotically, laughing till the soldiers and Jack were laughing helplessly too!

A sharp voice came from hehind them. It was their captain. They jumped to attention at once.

'Why waste time on this boy?' said the captain. 'You can see he is a circus boy, with a parrot like that! Search the van!'

Jack knew enough of the Hessian language now to understand roughly what the captain had said. *He* wasn't suspected then – and it was obvious that none of the soldiers suspected Philip or the girls. Now there was only Gussy left. Would he play up and be sensible?

Two soldiers went into Ma's van. They saw Gussy at once, sitting beside Ma. 'Who's this?' they said, sharply. 'What's her name?'

26

The pedlar's van

Gussy looked shyly up at them, and then hid his face in Ma's lap, as if very overcome. That had been Ma's idea, of course!

'Now, now!' said Ma, in Tauri-Hessian, tapping Gussy. 'Sit up and answer the gentlemen, my little Anna-Maria!' She turned to the soldiers.

'You must pardon her,' she said. 'She is a silly little girl, and cannot say boo to a goose! Sit up, my pet, and show these kind gentlemen what you are making.

Gussy sat up, and held out a piece of embroidery to the two soldiers, keeping his head down as if very shy indeed. Jack, looking in through the window, was amazed at Gussy's acting. And that embroidery! How very very clever of Ma to give Gussy that to show to the soldiers! He had seen Ma working on it herself, night after night!

'She is my favourite grandchild,' Ma prattled on. 'The prettiest little thing and so good. Talk to the kind gentlemen, Anna-Maria! Say how do you do.'

'I cannot,' said Gussy, and hid his face in Ma's lap again.

'Don't bother her,' said one soldier. 'I have a little girl at home as shy as she is. It's better to have them that way than bold and cheeky. How pretty her hair is! You must be proud of her, old woman.'

'She is such a good little needlewoman,' said Ma, proudly, and patted Gussy's head. 'Sit up, my pet – the gentlemen won't eat you!'

'We're going,' said the first soldier. 'Here, give her this to spend. She really does remind me of my little girl at home.'

He threw a coin to Ma and she caught it deftly and pocketed it at once. Jack heaved an enormous sigh of relief when he saw the two men walking away. He poked his head in at the window.

'It's all right. They've gone. Gussy, you were absolutely marvellous! Talk about an actor! Why, you're a born actor! A shy little girl to the life.'

Gussy lifted his head from Ma's lap. His eyes were bright and his face was red. He was laughing.

'It was Ma's idea, to behave like that,' he said. 'She said I must not show my face at all, I must be shy and put it into her lap.'

'A really good idea,' said Jack, and grinned at Ma's smiling face. 'Honestly, Gussy, I congratulate you – I never imagined you could act like that.'

'I like acting,' said Gussy. 'But not in girls' clothes.

I feel silly. Still – it was a very good idea. Now – I am safe, is it not so?'

'I think so,' said Jack, looking up the road. 'The men are going back to their cars. They are getting into them. Yes – the first car is going off. Whew! I was in a stew when those two fellows walked into your van.'

As soon as three military cars had shot off down the road, Philip left the bears' van, and came running over to the others, grinning. They all collected round Ma's van, and heard Jack's recital of Gussy's marvellous performance.

Gussy was pleased. He was not often praised by the others, and it was very pleasant to have them admiring him for once in a way. Then he caught sight of himself in Ma's mirror, ribbons and all, and his face clouded.

'I do not like myself,' he said, staring in the mirror. 'I will now dress in my own things again.'

'Oh no – not yet!' said Jack, quickly. 'You don't know who might recognize you suddenly if you did. You'll have to be a girl until we get you to safety somewhere. Go on, now, Gussy – you like acting. You'll give a marvellous performance!'

The vans went on again. The excitement quickly died down, and everyone grew silent. They were tired with their short night and the disturbances they had had. They stopped for a snack about six o'clock and then went on again.

They were now on a lonely country road. The surface

was bad, and the vans had to go slowly. Nobody minded that. Circus folk were never in a hurry except when their show was about to begin. Then everyone fell into a tremendous rush, and raced about in excitement.

They camped that night in the hills. They all slept very soundly to make up for the lack of sleep the night before. Then they set out again, jogging on slowly, not really very certain where they were going.

The Boss suddenly decided that they had taken a wrong turning a few miles back. The vans were turned round and back they all went, grumbling hard. They passed few people on the road, for they were now in a very lonely part.

'I want shops,' grumbled Ma. 'I need to buy things. We all need to buy things. We must go to some place where there are shops. I will go to tell the Boss.'

But she didn't, because she was afraid of him. She just went on grumbling. She wanted new cotton reels. She wanted some tinned fruit. She wanted hairpins.

'Cheer up, Ma – we may meet a travelling pedlar van,' said Pedro, getting tired of Ma's grumbling.

'What's that?' asked Jack.

'Oh – a van that takes all kinds of things to lonely villages,' said Pedro. 'I don't expect we *shall* meet one – but I've got to say something to keep Ma quiet!'

The Boss gave the order to camp early that night, and everyone was thankful. Soon fires were burning by the roadside and good smells came on the air.

Just as it was getting dusk, a small van came labouring up the hill on the slope of which the camp had been pitched. Madame Fifi saw it first and gave a shout.

Everyone looked up. 'Ma! You're in luck!' called Pedro. 'Here's a pedlar's van!'

The little black van drew up at the sight of the circus camp. Two men sat in the front of it, in the usual Tauri-Hessian clothes, sunburnt fellows, one small, one big and burly.

'Better keep out of sight, Gussy,' said Jack, suddenly. 'You never know – this might be men sent to check over the camp again.'

'Oh dear!' sighed Lucy-Ann. 'Don't say they're going to search all over again.'

The small man jumped out, went to the side of the van, and swung down half the wooden side, making a kind of counter. Inside the van, on shelves, were goods of every conceivable kind! Tins of meat, sardines and fruit. Tins of salmon and milk. Skeins of wool, reels of cotton, rolls of lace, bales of cheap cotton cloth. Safety-pins and hairpins. Combs of all kinds. Soap. Sweets. Really, it was just like a little general shop seen in so many villages.

'It sells everything!' said Pedro. 'Ma, do you want me to buy half the things for you?'

'No. I'll come myself,' said Ma, who enjoyed a bit of shopping. 'Stay here, Anna-Maria!'

'Can we go and have a look at the shop, do you think?' asked Dinah. 'You've got some Hessian money, haven't you, Jack? I do really want to buy some soap, and a few other things. Surely that van is genuine – those men can't be spies, sent to search the camp again!'

'No. I don't think they can be,' said Jack. 'The van does seem quite genuine, as you say. All right – we'll go and buy a few things. Not Gussy, though.'

So, while the others strolled off in the dusk to the little travelling shop, poor Gussy was left behind in Ma's van. He was very cross.

The small man sold all the goods. The big man merely helped, handing down this and that, and wrapping up anything that needed it. He said nothing at all. The other man was a real talker. He chattered all the time, chaffed the women, and passed on little bits of news.

'And what news have *you* got?' he asked Ma and old Lucia, as he sold them hairpins and combs. 'You've come from the direction of Borken, haven't you? Any news of the King there? He's not been found yet, you know!'

Ma gave him her news, and described the clamour of the bells in the night. Old Lucia chimed in with a few remarks too.

'Where's little Prince Aloysius?' she wanted to know. 'They say he was sent to school in England. If the King is dead, the little Prince will have to be brought back, won't he?'

'We had soldiers searching our camp today,' said Madame Fifi. 'Though what they expected to find, I don't know. The King perhaps!'

Everyone laughed. The chattering and buying went on for some time, and the pedlars did very well. Jack went up to buy some sweets for the girls, Kiki on his shoulder.

'Good morning, good night, good gracious!' said Kiki, conversationally, to the pedlar who was serving. He laughed. But the other man didn't. He turned round and looked very sharply at Kiki indeed. Jack felt uncomfortable. Why did the second man look round like that? He tried to see what he was like, but it was now dark, and difficult to see inside the little van.

Lucy-Ann pointed to some toffee. 'I'd like some of that,' she said, in English. Jack saw the man at the back of the van stiffen. He seemed to be listening for what Lucy-Ann might say next. He reached up to a shelf, took down a tin, and then stood still again, as Lucy-Ann spoke once more.

'Let's have a tin of pineapple. Kiki likes that.'

The man swung round. Jack hurriedly pushed Lucy-Ann back into the darkness. This fellow was a spy! He was sure of it! He took another look at him, but could not make out very much. A head of black, curly hair, such as all the Tauri-Hessians had – a small black moustache – that was about all Jack could see.

'What's up, Jack?' said Lucy-Ann, in astonishment as he hurried her away from the van, pulling Dinah and Philip with him too.

He told them hurriedly what he thought and they were very worried. They rushed back to Ma's van to see if

Gussy was all right. To their great relief, he was there, looking very cross. 'Though why we should think he wouldn't be there, I don't know,' said Jack. 'Gussy, get out your embroidery. We've seen somebody suspicious. He heard Lucy-Ann talking in English, and Kiki too, and he was *much* too interested!'

'Well – we'll hope he clears off soon,' said Philip. 'I'll go and watch, and tell you when they're gone.'

But the pedlar's van didn't go! The two men shut up the side of the van, safely locking up all their goods, and then sat outside with a little camp fire, cooking some kind of meal.

'They're staying the night,' reported Philip. 'Not too good, is it? And Madame Fifi told me that the small man has been asking questions about Kiki – if the boy who owns her belongs to the camp – and where his caravan is!'

'Blow!' said Jack. 'What can we do? We can't possibly run away. I've no idea at all where we are – miles away from anywhere, that's certain! Well – we can only hope for the best. We'll sleep as usual under the girls' van, and Gussy can be with Ma. After all, he's the important one – we're not really important, except that Gussy escaped with us, and presumably the Count will think that wherever we are, Gussy will be too!'

The girls went to their van and undressed to go to sleep. Gussy was safely with Ma. The three boys lay on the rugs below the girls' van as usual. Pedro soon fell asleep, but Jack and Philip were worried, and lay awake, whispering.

Suddenly Jack clutched Philip. 'I can hear someone,' he whispered, in his ear. 'Someone crawling near this van.'

Jack sat up cautiously and felt for his torch. Yes – someone *was* near the van, crawling quietly on all fours. Jack flicked on his torch at once.

A surprised face was caught in the light. A man was on hands and knees nearby. It was the big pedlar from the little van! His black hair showed up plainly in the beam of the torch.

'What do you want?' said Jack, fiercely. 'What do you mean by crawling around like this? I'll raise the camp, and have them all after you!'

27

A surprise – and a plan

'Sh!' said the man, urgently. 'I . . .'

And then, before he could say another word, a very strange thing happened! Kiki, who had been watching the man in greatest surprise, suddenly spread her wings and flew to his shoulder! She rubbed her beak against his cheek in the most loving manner, crooning like a dove.

'Kiki!' said the man, and stroked her neck.

'Silly-Bill,' said Kiki, lovingly. 'Silly-Billy, put the kettle on, send for the doctor!'

Jack was so astonished that he simply couldn't say a word. Why in the world was Kiki behaving like that – and how did this man know her? It was Philip who guessed. He suddenly rolled himself over on hands and knees, and crawled at top speed from under the wagon.

'Bill! BILL! This must be a dream! Bill, it *is* you, isn't it? Are you wearing a wig?'

With a grin, the big man stripped off the whole of his black hair – yes, he was wearing a wig! And without it he looked himself at once, in spite of the little black moustache which, of course, was merely stuck on.

'Bill, oh, Bill! I can't believe it!' said Philip. Bill put out his great hand and the two shook hands solemnly for quite a long time. Then Jack joined them, his eyes almost falling out of his head. It must be a dream! This *couldn't* be real!

But it was. It was Bill himself. He asked eagerly about the girls. 'I was so relieved to see them both looking so well,' he said. 'Though I hardly knew them in that get-up they were wearing. But I knew Lucy-Ann's clear high voice all right – and I spotted Kiki too, of course. I couldn't believe it when I saw her on your shoulder, Jack. I really couldn't. Where are the girls? In this van here?'

'Yes. We heard that you had made enquiries about where our van was,' said Jack. 'And we thought you were spies! We didn't guess it was you, and that you wanted to come and find us in the night. Let's get into the van and wake the girls. We'll wake old Pedro too. He's a great friend of ours.'

Soon an extremely excited company of six people and a parrot sat in Pedro's little van. Lucy-Ann hung on to Bill and wouldn't let him move even an inch from her. Tears ran down her cheeks and she kept brushing them away.

'I can't help it, Bill, I'm not really crying, it's just because I'm so happy again, I just can't help it, Bill!' said poor Lucy-Ann, laughing through the tears that simply poured down her face.

Bill took out an enormous hanky and patted her eyes. He was very fond of Lucy-Ann. 'You make me think of Gussy,' he said, 'and the time when Philip took a kitchen tablecloth to dry *his* tears! Cheer up – we're all together again – and you can give me most valuable information!'

'How's Mother?' said Philip. 'Is she very worried?'

'Very!' said Bill. 'She and I were caught and tied up the night you were kidnapped. We couldn't get free. We had to wait till Mrs Gump came along the road next morning on her way to the cottage, and call out to her. By that time, of course, all trace of you had been lost. We've had the police hunting every county in England for you! We didn't dare to say Gussy had gone too, because we didn't want the news to get to the Tauri-Hessians.'

'We went off in a plane, after a car had taken us away,' said Philip. 'Jack hid in the boot of the car and then stowed away in the plane – so he knew where we had gone. We were imprisoned in Borken Castle with Gussy – and Jack managed to rescue us!'

'I joined this circus with Kiki,' explained Jack. 'Pedro was a brick – he helped me no end. We got Toni and Bingo the acrobats to help in the rescue – phew, it was pretty dangerous!'

He told Bill all about it. Bill listened in amazement. These children! The things that happened to them – the way they tackled everything that came along, and never turned a hair. And now they had got Gussy safely with them, disguised as a girl!

227

'But Bill – you haven't told us what *you're* doing here,' said Jack. 'Fancy you coming along in a pedlar's van – all dressed up as a Tauri-Hessian – really, it's too amazing to be true.'

'Well, it's true all right,' said Bill. 'You see, when our Government learnt that the King of Tauri-Hessia had been captured – or killed, for all we know – it was absolutely essential that we should find out whether this was true or not – and it was essential we should find Gussy too, if possible. So, as the Tauri-Hessian Government had put Gussy into my charge, as you know, it was decided that I should be the one to come out and make inquiries.'

'I see – spy round to see how the land lay,' said Philip. 'Did you think we might all be in Tauri-Hessia?'

'Yes – I came to the conclusion that wherever Gussy had been taken, you should be there too – to be held as hostages, if our own Government made any trouble about Gussy,' said Bill. 'And as soon as the news came that the King had disappeared, we felt sure that Gussy would be somewhere in Borken, Count Paritolen's own territory – and possibly the King might be held prisoner there too – so I and another man, who speaks Tauri-Hessian well, flew over straight away to do a spot of spying. Hence the pedlar's van!'

'Mother will be feeling awfully worried, with you gone too,' said Dinah.

'I'll get a message through to her sometime tomorrow,'

said Bill. 'Now, I wonder if you can tell me something – have you any sort of an idea at all where the King might be hidden?'

'In Borken Castle,' said Jack, promptly. 'I'm sure of it! I'll tell you why.'

He told Bill of how he had explored the castle – and how he had overheard the Count and Madame Tatiosa talking excitedly together. 'That was the night before the King was known to have disappeared,' said Jack. 'I think their plans were going well – probably they even had him a prisoner somewhere then. And the obvious place to take him would be the Count's own castle – he would then have Gussy there – and the King too – right under his hand! He could bargain with both, if he wanted to.'

Bill listened to this long speech with the greatest interest. 'I think you're right,' he said. 'I wish we could get into the castle and find out something. Ronald, the fellow who is with me, speaks the language fluently. I wonder if he could bluff his way in – say he's a tradesman come to do a repair, or something.'

'*I* know what he could do,' said Jack, with a sudden surge of excitement. 'I know a way in, Bill – the way I got out the first night I was there! It leads through secret passages up to the big ballroom. There's a way into the ballroom from behind a great picture. I don't know how to move the picture away, though – so as to get into the ballroom. That's the snag.'

'We'll find out!' said Bill. 'Jack, this is great! Are you

229

game to come with me – and Ronald too, my pal – and show us the way into the castle? If only we could find out whether the King is alive or not – or whether he's a prisoner – it would be a great help. There's one thing, the plans of the plotters must be greatly upset now that Gussy has gone! No King for the country – and no Prince to set in his place! Very difficult for them!'

'I'll come, Bill,' said Jack, his face red with excitement.

'I'll come too,' said Philip.

'No – you must stay and keep an eye on the girls,' said Bill. 'I must have one of you with them. Keep an eye on Gussy too. Pedro can help there.'

'Shall we go now?' asked Jack, eagerly. 'It's a very dark night.'

'The sooner the better,' said Bill, and got up. 'Wait here. I'll fetch Ronnie. I'll have to tell him a few things first though! My word, he'll be astonished!'

Bill disappeared. For a moment the five said nothing. Kiki broke the silence. 'Ding dong bell, Billy's in the well,' she said. 'Pussy's got a cold – a-chooo!'

'Idiot!' said Jack. 'My word – what a night! Fancy BILL turning up here. It was Kiki who recognized him when he came crawling round the van. I didn't.'

'Everything will be all right now,' said Lucy-Ann. 'It always is when Bill comes.'

'Don't talk too soon,' said Dinah. 'They've not got an easy job tonight!'

Bill came back with Ronnie, who seemed rather overcome at meeting so many people at once. He had much more to say as a pedlar than with Bill in Pedro's van!

'Well – are we ready?' said Bill. 'Come on then.'

They slipped out of the caravan, and Jack followed the two men. Their van was quite near, and Jack guessed what they were going to do. They were going to drive back to Borken. It wouldn't take long, because it wasn't really very far away. The circus procession of horse-drawn vans had gone at a walking pace the last two days, and had once had to retrace their steps as well. It wouldn't take more than an hour to get to Borken.

They went off in the night, Ronnie driving. Kiki was on Jack's shoulder. She meant to be in everything, no matter what it was!

They came to Borken. The town was in utter darkness. 'Park the van in the field where the camp was,' said Jack, and guided them to it. 'The castle is only just up the steep slope of the hill then.'

They parked the van behind a big bush. Then they made their way up the steep slope to the castle. 'There's the bell tower,' said Jack, as they came nearer. 'Better go cautiously in case there are people on guard. The Count must know that we escaped by means of the bell tower. We had to leave Toni's wire rope behind, stretched from tower to tower.'

Nobody seemed to be about, however. But Jack suddenly saw lights in the castle windows high above them. They blazed out of half a dozen windows – something was going on in the castle in the middle of that night, it was certain!

'We might be able to have a look in on that,' said Bill, staring at the lights. 'Must be some kind of a conference going on.'

'There's a hole in one of the walls of the conference room – at least, I think it must be a conference room,' said Jack, suddenly excited. 'I saw a round table, and chairs, and writing pads and pencils all set out. If we could get up to that room, and look through the hole, we might see something interesting – and hear something too!'

'We might,' agreed Bill. 'Come on – let's get going. Into the bell tower we go! Where's that trap door you told us about?'

They were soon in the bell tower. Jack searched about for the trap door. He found it, and Bill pulled it open. Down they went into the little cellar below. Bill pulled the trap door shut behind him.

'Lead the way, Jack,' he said, and flashed on an extremely powerful torch. With a jump Jack saw that both men now carried revolvers too. Gosh – this might be a serious business then!

'This way,' said Jack, and stepped over the junk in the underground hole. 'Better be as quiet as we can. Now – through here!'

28

To Borken Castle again!

Jack clambered through the round hole at the other end of the little cellar. He was now in the very narrow, low-roofed passage he remembered so well, because he had had to walk through it with his head well bent. He led Bill and Ronnie up the steeply sloping way, lit by Bill's powerful torch.

Jack stopped when they came to the top of the long, sloping passage. 'We're very near the room where the spy-hole is,' he whispered. 'If there is a conference being held – or some sort of meeting – we'll be able to look through the hole at it – or you will, Bill, because as far as I know there's only one hole.'

'Let me know when we come to it,' whispered Bill, and they went on again. In a short while Jack saw a little beam of light coming from the side of the right-hand wall – that must be the spyhole!

He whispered to Bill. Bill saw the beam of light and nodded. There was not room for him to get in front of

Jack, so the boy went on past the little spyhole, and let Bill stand by it behind him. Ronnie was by Bill, quite silent. Kiki had been tapped on the beak, so she knew she was to be quiet too.

Bill glued his eye to the spyhole. He saw the same room that Jack had seen – a room with a round table, chairs pulled up to it, and writing materials on the table.

But now there were lights blazing in the room – and every chair at the table was filled. At the top sat Count Paritolen. Beside him sat his sister, Madame Tatiosa. On his other side sat someone else, whom Bill knew from photographs – the Prime Minister, husband of Madame Tatiosa. He looked ill at ease and grave. Men in military uniform were also round the table.

At the bottom of the table stood a tall man, with a great likeness to Gussy – his uncle, the King! Bill heaved a sigh of relief. So he hadn't been killed. Well, that was one good thing at any rate. If only he could be got away, things could be put right very quickly, and civil war would be avoided.

Bill strained his ears to hear what was going on. He could not hear very well, behind the wooden panelling, but he heard enough to know what was happening.

The King was being urged to abdicate – to leave his throne, go into retirement, and let Gussy – the Prince Aloysius – rule in his stead.

'If you will not sign this document of abdication, then

it will be the worse for you,' finished Count Paritolen. 'You will, I fear, not be heard of again.'

Bill followed this with difficulty, for he did not speak Tauri-Hessian well. He had, in fact, only tried to learn it when he knew he might have to go to the country. But he had no doubt that that was what the Count was saying.

The Prime Minister said something in protest, but the Count would not listen. Madame Tatiosa made a short, angry speech and sat down. The King bowed, and then spoke in such a low voice that Bill couldn't hear a word.

'Very well,' said the Count. 'You may have tonight to make up your mind – tonight only. We will adjourn this meeting.'

He stood up and so did everyone else. The Count went out with his sister and the Prime Minister. The King followed, closely hemmed in by four men. He looked sad and worried.

The lights in the conference room dimmed, and there was silence. Bill turned to Ronnie and repeated rapidly what he had seen and what he thought had happened.

'As far as I can make out the King's got tonight to think things over. If he says no, he *won't* give up the throne, that's the end of him. I think he will say no.'

There was a silence behind the wooden panelling for a moment or two. Bill debated with himself. Could he get back to the capital of Tauri-Hessia, tell what he had seen, and bring men to rescue the King?

No – there wouldn't be time – the capital town was

too far off. There was only one sure thing to do – and that was to see if he himself could get the King away.

He whispered this to Jack. The boy nodded. 'Yes. If only we knew where he was going to be tonight! He won't be put into the tower room, I'm sure. They'd be afraid he'd escape too, like Gussy. Let's go to the ballroom, where that moving picture hangs – we might be able to shove it aside and get into the room.'

He led the way again – up some very steep steps, up and up. Then round a sharp corner and into a narrow, dark passage running just inside the walls of the rooms, but a little below the level of the floor. Then came a small flight of steps, and Jack paused.

'These are the steps that lead up to that picture,' he whispered. 'You must see if you can find out how to move it away from the hole, Bill – it slides right away from it, keeping level with the wall.'

Bill and Ronnie began to feel about all over the place. Bill suddenly found a knob. Ah – this must be it! A pull at this might set the mechanism working that moved the picture away, and left a hole in its place.

He listened carefully. No noise came from the room within. Well – he'd have to risk it, anyhow. Bill pulled the knob.

Nothing happened. He twisted it. Still nothing happened. Then he pushed it – and it gave beneath his hand.

Then came a slight scraping noise, and it seemed to Bill as if part of the wall was disappearing! But it was only the picture moving to one side, leaving a hole almost as large as itself – the secret entrance to the ballroom!

There was very little light in the big room – merely a dim glow from a lamp whose wick had been turned down. Bill peered out.

'No one here,' he whispered to the others. 'We'll get into the room while we can.'

He climbed out of the hole and jumped lightly to the floor. The others followed. Their rubber shoes made no sound.

'We'd better just go and *see* if the King has been put into the tower room,' whispered Jack. 'I'll go. I know the way. You stay here – behind these curtains.'

He sped into the anteroom, and saw the spiral stair-way. He stopped and listened. No sound anywhere. He ran up the steps quietly and came to the little landing. He flashed his torch on the door that led into the room where Philip and the others had been imprisoned.

It was wide open! The room beyond was dark, too, so it was plain that the King was not imprisoned there. Jack went down again.

He tiptoed to the curtains behind which Bill and Ronnie were hiding. 'No good,' he whispered. 'The door's wide open. He's not there.'

'Listen!' said Bill, suddenly. 'I can hear something!'

They listened. It was the clump-clump of marching feet. They came nearer and nearer. It sounded like two or three people. Bill peeped round the side of the curtain when the sound had passed by.

'Two soldiers,' he whispered. 'They must have gone to relieve two others on guard somewhere – and who should they be guarding but the King? We'll wait and see if two others come back this way, then we shall know the first two have gone on guard somewhere – and we'll explore down that passage, where the first two went.'

'When I was here before, the sentry on guard kept disappearing down there,' said Jack, remembering. 'It's a kind of sentry beat, I think. Perhaps the King has been taken down there and locked into a cell.'

'Listen!' said Ronnie. Back came marching feet again and two different sentries went by smartly in the opposite direction from the others, and disappeared. The three could hear the sound of their feet for some time, and then no more.

'Now!' said Bill. 'And keep your ears open and your eyes peeled too.'

They all went down the dark passage where the two first sentries had gone. Right down to the end – round a sharp-angled turn, and down a few steps – along a narrower passage, and round another turn. But here they stopped. They could hear marching feet again – coming nearer!

There was a room opening off near where the three stood. Bill pushed open the door and the three went into it hurriedly. It was quite dark. Bill switched his torch on for a moment and they saw that it was a kind of box-room. The sentries passed right by it, went a good way up the passage and then, stamp-stamp, they turned and came back again.

Bill listened to their feet marching. They seemed to go a long way down the passage, a long, long way, before they turned to come back. 'I should think the King must be locked up somewhere about the middle of their sentry-go,' said Bill. 'We'll let them come up here once more, and when they have gone right past us, up to the other end of their beat, we'll slip down here and explore a bit. We can always go and hide beyond the other end of their walk, if we hear them coming back.'

The sentries came marching back, passed the three hidden in the little box room again, and went on to the end of their beat. Bill, Ronnie and Jack slipped quickly out of the box room and ran lightly down the passage. They turned a corner and came to a dead end. A stout door faced them, well and truly bolted – and locked too, as Bill found when he tried to open it!

'Sssst!' said Ronnie, suddenly, and pulled them back into a dark corner. Bill and Jack wondered what had scared him – then they saw!

A door was opening silently opposite to them – a door they hadn't seen because it was part of the panelling itself. Someone came through carrying a lamp. It was the Count Paritolen. Had he come to kill the King? Or to try once more to persuade him to give up his throne?

Bill saw something else. He saw what the Count was holding – a big key! The key to the King's room, no doubt!

The Count heard the sentries coming back and went back through the hidden door, closing it softly. He evidently meant to wait till the sentries had come up and then had gone back again.

'Ronnie,' said Bill, his mouth close to his friend's ear, 'we get that key, do you understand? And we get the Count too. Will you tackle him while I open the door and find out if the King's there? He mustn't make any noise.'

'He won't,' said Ronnie, grimly. The sentries came right up, and then turned, stamp-stamp, and went back again. As soon as they had turned the first corner, the hidden door opened again, and the Count stepped through swiftly, lamp in one hand, key in the other.

Everything happened so quickly then that Jack was bewildered. He heard an exclamation from the Count, and then he saw Bill running to the door with the key, and Ronnie dragging the Count hurriedly back through the hidden door. The lamp went out. There was complete silence.

Ronnie came back and switched on his torch. He saw Bill unlocking the door and pulling back bolts. 'I found a nice little cell back there,' he said, jerking his head towards the door. 'Just right for the Count. He's tied up and he can shout the place down if he likes – nobody can hear him in that room!'

'Good work,' said Bill. 'Blow these bolts – there are half a dozen of them! We'll have the sentries back here before we know where we are!'

Ronnie blew out the passage lamp that shone near the door. 'Don't want the sentries to see the bolts are drawn!' he said. 'Buck up, Bill. They're coming back. Jack and I will wait here – just in *case* there's trouble with the sentries. Do buck up!'

29

An exciting time

Bill at last got the door open and went in. A shaft of light shone out from the room at once. Ronnie shut the door quickly. Jack found that his heart was beginning to thump again. Those sentries – would they come back before Bill had got the King?

The door opened again, but this time no shaft of light showed. Bill had turned out the lamp inside the room. Someone was with him – the King. Oh, good! thought Jack.

The sentries were coming back. Their feet could be clearly heard. Bill hurried the King across to the hidden door, opened it and pushed him through. Ronnie followed, and then Jack.

Just in time! 'Do you suppose they'll see the door is unbolted?' said Jack. 'You didn't have time to bolt it.'

'We'll soon know!' said Bill. 'I'm afraid they *will* notice it – it's their job to check up on that, I'm sure.'

Jack suddenly gave a little cry. 'Kiki! Where is she? She

was on my shoulder a minute ago, now she's gone. I never felt her fly off in my excitement. Oh, Bill – she must be out there in the passage somewhere.'

She was – and she was very much annoyed to find that Jack seemed to have disappeared. Where was he? She could hear the sentries coming nearer and nearer, and the sound of their clump-clump-clumping annoyed her.

She flew up to a jutting-out stone in the wall, and when the two men marched just below her, she hooted long and loud.

'HOOOOOO! HOOO-HOOO-HOOO!'

The sound of marching feet stopped abruptly. One of the men said something quickly to the other in a frightened voice.

Kiki yapped like a dog and then snarled. It sounded most extraordinary in that dark, echoing passage. The men looked all round. Where was the dog?

'Mee-ow-ow-ow!' wailed Kiki, like a hungry cat, and then went off into a cackle of laughter.

'Wipe your feet, blow your nose, pop goes the weasel, pop-pop-pop!'

The men didn't understand a word, of course, but that frightened them all the more. They clutched each other, feeling the hairs on their head beginning to prickle in fright.

Kiki coughed and cleared her throat in a remarkably human way. Why that should have put the two sentries into an absolute panic she couldn't guess! But it certainly did, and, casting their rifles away, they fled down the passage at top speed, howling out something in their own language.

Jack had heard all this, for he had opened the hidden door a little, feeling anxious about Kiki. He listened to her performance with a grin. Good old Kiki! He called her softly and she flew down to his shoulder in delight.

Bill wondered what would be the best thing to do now. It would be dangerous to go back the way they had come, because the scared sentries would certainly arrive back with others to probe into the mystery of the hooting and barking and mewing and coughing!

'I wonder if the passage behind this hidden door leads anywhere except to the room you put the Count in,' said Bill to Ronnie.

'We'll go and ask him,' said Ronnie, cheerfully. 'I'll poke this in his ribs and see if he'll talk.' 'This' was his revolver. Bill laughed.

'You won't need that. He'll talk all right when he sees the King here. Your Majesty, perhaps *you* would like to deal with the Count, and command him to show us the way out?'

The King could talk perfect English. Like Gussy, he had been sent to England to be educated. He nodded, his eyes gleaming. It was obvious that he would certainly enjoy a few words with the Count!

They went to the cell-like room into which Ronnie had shoved the Count, locking him in, nicely tied up.

Count Paritolen was on the floor, looking furious. When he saw the King he looked so thunderstruck that Bill laughed.

'Undo his legs, Ronnie, but not his arms,' said Bill. 'He should stand up politely before the King.'

The Count's legs were untied and he stood up, his face very pale indeed. The King began to address him in vigorous Tauri-Hessian. The Count wilted – his head hung forward – and finally he fell on his knees, a picture of misery and fright. The King touched him contemptuously with his foot, and said a few more words. The Count got up again, and said, 'Ai! Ai! Ai!' eagerly, which Jack knew to mean 'Yes! Yes! Yes!'

'He's going to show us the way out,' said Bill. 'Good thing too. I seem to hear a tremendous noise starting up somewhere in the distance. No doubt our friends the sentries have brought all their buddies along – and have discovered the unbolted door and the empty room. Tell the Count to get a move on, Ronnie.'

With his arms still tied behind him the Count stumbled out of the little bare room. He led them to a door opposite and kicked it open. A small stairway led downwards. 'I'll go first,' said Ronnie, and nipped in front of the Count.

The steps led down to a little panelled room, rather like a small study. The Count said a few words, nodding his head at a panel. Ronnie stepped forward and slid the panel downwards. A hole just big enough for a man to squeeze through was now showing. Nothing could be seen the other side because something was hanging over it.

'Tapestry hangings,' said Bill, and knocked his hand against it. 'Well, well – nice lot of hidey-holes and secrets you've got here, Count. Very nice indeed. What do we do next? Get behind this tapestry?'

'He says it's tapestry hanging in one of the bedrooms,' said Ronnie. 'If we make our way behind it a bit, we'll come to an opening. Here goes!'

He went through the hole, and made his way behind endless tapestry that hung loose from ceiling to floor. At last he came to where, as the Count had said, there was an opening. It was where two different pieces of tapestry met. Ronnie poked his way between them and found himself in a bedroom. He saw beautiful furniture and carpets as he flashed his torch round. The room was quite empty.

The others came out into the room too, having made their way behind the tapestry. Jack sneezed because it was full of dust. Kiki promptly sneezed too, much to the Count's amazement. He had not met Kiki before!

'Now where?' said Ronnie, digging his revolver into the Count's ribs quite suddenly. The man gave a startled jump and almost fell over in fright.

'I hardly think that poke in the ribs was necessary,' said Bill, with a grin.

'No, not necessary – but awfully good for a nasty little

double-crosser like him!' said Ronnie. 'People who threaten others with this, that and the other when they are in power deserve a bit of a fright from my gun. Now then, Count – the quickest and best way out, please!'

This last was said in Tauri-Hessian and the Count replied at once, his words tumbling over one another in his desire to please this fierce Englishman.

'It's easy now,' said Ronnie. 'We apparently go down the back stairs into the deserted kitchen quarters, and just let ourselves out of the back door. Nothing could be simpler!'

So down the back stairs they went, and into a vast kitchen. Three cats were there, their eyes gleaming in the light of Bill's torch. Kiki yapped like a small dog, and the cats fled into corners at once.

'Kiki!' said Jack, with a laugh. 'You're irrepressible!'

Kiki tried to repeat the word and couldn't. Bill was now unlocking the great back door. They all went out into a big yard. Then down to the castle gate, a massive wrought iron affair, whose keys hung most conveniently at the side. Bill unlocked the gate and out they went, finding themselves in the main street of Borken.

'Now – where is the place we left the van?' wondered Bill. 'Jack, could you take Ronnie to it? Ronnie, we'll wait here for you.'

Jack sped off with Ronnie. He had been in the town several times and knew the way. He and Ronnie were soon in the field where they had left the van, and Ronnie started it up at once.

It was not long before the van drew up beside the other three in the dark highway. They got in. Bill was behind with the Count and Jack. The King went in front with Ronnie. It was queer to sit in the back, with all kinds of goods rattling on the shelves. The Count, however, took no notice. He was feeling extremely gloomy.

'I say – where are we going? This isn't the way back to the circus camp,' said Jack, suddenly.

'No, I know,' said Bill. 'I'm afraid we must go straight to the capital town of Tauri-Hessia, Jack – the King needs to be there at the earliest possible moment. Things are in a great turmoil, you see – nobody knows what is going to happen – no King – no Prince – the Count apparently trying to take things over – the Prime Minister a weak tool . . .'

'Yes, I see,' said Jack. 'But as soon as the King appears, everything will be all right, won't it?'

'It will certainly be all right after he has appeared to his people and spoken to them,' said Bill. 'He will have quite a lot of interesting things to tell them! I think, too, it is essential that Gussy should appear also – so that the people will be sure that he and his uncle are on good terms, and back each other up.'

'Oh, Gussy will love that!' said Jack. 'Do we go back to get him?'

'We do,' said Bill. 'And we also get the others. I'm sure

the King will want to see Gussy's fellow prisoners. He has a lot to hear about, you know.'

The King certainly wanted to meet all the others when he heard the amazing story that Bill had to tell him. It was all told when they reached the Palace. Then, after a delighted and amazed welcome from a few servants on duty, the King retired to a little room with Bill, Ronnie and Jack. The Count was sent off in disgrace with four soldiers in front of him and four behind!

'Left, right, left, right!' shouted Kiki after him. 'God save the King!'

It was still dark, for the sun was not due to rise for another hour. Jack suddenly yawned. He really couldn't help it.

'You'd better have a snooze,' said Bill. 'The King is sending his State Car to fetch the others first thing in the morning. He will lend you some of Gussy's clothes, he says, if you want to look decent. The others are being sent clothes too, especially, of course, Gussy. He couldn't possibly appear in his girls' things!'

'This is going to be fun from now on,' said Jack, trying to keep awake. 'Oh, gosh, I'm sleepy. What are you going to do, Bill? Have a sleep, too?'

'No. I'm going to get in touch with your aunt by radio,' said Bill, 'and tell her you're all safe. I'll get her to fly out tomorrow, and we'll all be together again!'

Jack fell on to a sofa, feeling that he couldn't keep awake one moment longer. 'Good old Bill,' he said.

'Everything comes right when you're here. Good morning – I mean good night!'

And in half a second more he was fast asleep. What a night he had had!

30

'God save the King!'

Jack awoke to find a pretty Tauri-Hessian maid bringing him a most magnificent breakfast. Somebody had undressed him, put silk pyjamas on him and popped him into a luxurious bed. He was amazed.

'To think they did all that and I never woke up!' he thought. 'I *must* have been tired! Gosh – what a breakfast! Kiki, look here – the biggest, juiciest grapefruit I ever did see in my life – and two halves, not one. You can have one for yourself if you don't make too much mess.'

Kiki approved of the grapefruit. She settled down to it, and for once in a way didn't say a word. Jack ate every scrap of the generous breakfast, and then lay back, thinking over the happenings of the night before.

'I bet the Count isn't eating a breakfast like this,' he told Kiki. 'What do *you* think?'

'The doctor's got a cold, fetch the King,' said Kiki, looking to see if Jack had left any of his grapefruit. 'One, two, how-do-you-do?'

'Buckle my shoe, you mean,' said Jack. '*I say* – look! Do you suppose those princely clothes are for me to put on, Kiki, old bird? Goodness, the Tauri-Hessians won't know if I'm the Prince, or Gussy.'

Bill came in, looking much smartened up. 'Oh, you're awake at last,' he said. 'My word, you don't mean to say you ate *all* that breakfast!'

'Kiki helped me,' said Jack, with a grin. 'Have the others been sent for yet, Bill?'

'Yes. I'd like to see their faces when the King's State Car rolls up, complete with clothes for them all,' said Bill. 'The King's a great sport. He's asked Pedro, Toni, Bingo and old Ma too – and sent clothes for them all!'

'Goodness!' said Jack. 'Old Ma! She'll have the time of her life. But if it hadn't been for her looking after Gussy he'd certainly have been caught. I say – this is going to be quite a party, isn't it?'

'Oh, quite,' said Bill. 'And your aunt is arriving today too!'

'It's just like a pantomime ending!' said Jack, delighted. 'Everyone on the stage at the end!'

'You'd better get up,' said Bill. 'The King is making his speech to the people at twelve o'clock, and it's now eleven. After that there is to be a really splendid luncheon laid on – and you'll be sorry you ate so much breakfast, I can tell you!'

Jack leapt out of bed. 'Is it really eleven o'clock? Gosh, I'll never be ready. I don't know how to put all these clothes on – buckles – sashes – ruffles – good gracious, is it royal dress?'

'No. Ordinary Tauri-Hessian festival wear,' said Bill. 'I don't feel able to cope with it myself, nor does Ronnie. We feel a bit more at ease in our own things, but you and the others will look fine.'

Jack was ready at a quarter to twelve. He looked at himself in the glass. 'Gracious – I'm like a theatrical prince. I really must have my photograph taken to show the boys at school – they'll be amazed!'

There came the sound of cheering in the street below. Jack opened his window and looked out. A very grand State Car was being driven slowly up the street, followed by yet another. The people were cheering each one as it went by.

Jack nearly fell out of the window, and Kiki gave a loud screech. 'Look, Kiki – do you see who's in the first car?' cried Jack. 'Lucy-Ann, Philip, Gussy and Dinah! Did you ever see anyone looking so grand? And look in the second car – Pedro – Ma – Toni and Bingo! They look as fine as if they were just going to perform in the circus ring!'

So they did. Ma, especially, looked magnificent, and she had a sudden unexpected dignity that made Pedro look at her with surprise and great pride. His mother! Old Ma, riding in a State Car, wearing silk clothes right down to her skin! Pedro couldn't believe it.

He looked very grand himself, and enjoyed it. He

knew that nothing like this would ever happen to him again in his life and he meant to enjoy every moment of it.

Toni and Bingo looked grand but subdued. They were not in the least nervous when they went into the circus ring – but they couldn't help feeling nervous now – all this cheering and shouting when they weren't even performing!

The cars turned in at the gates, and Jack leaned out of the window and yelled, quite forgetting that he was in a King's palace.

'Lucy-Ann! I'm up here!'

Kiki squawked too. 'Hip-hip-hip-hip-hurrah! Send for the doctor!'

Twelve o'clock came. The King went out on the balcony of his palace to show himself to his people and to make a speech to explain all that had happened. There was dead silence as the loud-speakers relayed the simple, vigorous speech.

Bill thought that Tauri-Hessia had a very fine King. He was glad that the Count had not dethroned him and put Gussy up as King himself. Gussy was just a timid little boy at present – but perhaps, when he had learnt all that his good school had to teach him, at lessons and at games, he would make as fine a King as his uncle.

Gussy had a tremendous reception when his uncle called him to his side, and presented him to the people.

After all the scares of the last few days, they needed to see not only the King but the little Prince too.

Gussy looked every inch a Prince, as he saluted stiffly, and then bowed in every direction. He wore magnificent clothes, and his cloak blew out in the wind, showing its scarlet lining. Jack grinned as he thought how Gussy had looked when he had seen him last – dressed as a girl, with his long hair tied up in bows. Poor Gussy! Nobody must ever learn of that, or he would be teased about it for the rest of his life – and Gussy did not like teasing.

The next thing was the luncheon. The children had all been put at a table together, with Gussy and Pedro as well. Ma, Toni and Bingo were at a side table too, very conscious of their fine clothes. They used fine manners to match, and ate everything with knives, forks or spoons, instead of using only their fingers half the time as they usually did.

The six children talked eagerly together, exchanging news. 'Fank is up and about again,' said Philip. 'Thank goodness he is, or I couldn't have come. Hallo, Snoozy, do you want to join us at last? He's seen those almonds, Dinah – do look at him, holding one and nibbling it!'

'I don't like him on the table,' said Dinah, but she was much too happy to make a fuss. She told Jack of the excitement when the message came that they were all to dress in State clothes and be driven to the Palace. 'We just couldn't believe it!' she said. 'Tell us again about last night, Jack, and how you rescued the King and caught the Count.'

Gussy was tremendously excited. His eyes sparkled, and he talked nineteen to the dozen. He felt in his element now – he was a Prince, the heir to the throne, Prince Aloysius Gramondie – not a timid little boy with a lot of long hair!

'Here's Aunt Allie!' cried Lucy-Ann, suddenly. She threw down her table-napkin and flew across the luncheon room, thinking of nothing but welcoming the person she loved so much. 'Aunt Allie! You've come!'

Mrs Cunningham was being ushered into the great room by two servants, who called out her name. Bill went to her at once, and Dinah, Philip and Jack joined Lucy-Ann in her rush across the room. This was all that was needed to make things perfect!

Bill's eyes were shining as he took his wife to introduce her to the King. A place had been left for her on his other side, for her aeroplane had been expected for the last half hour. She was quite bewildered by everything, for she knew only half the story, of course.

Gussy waited till the others had made enough fuss of her and then went up himself. She held out her hand to him, and he bowed over it, and kissed it politely, just as his uncle had done. Somehow it seemed right in Tauri-Hessia – quite a natural thing to do, and none of the children even thought of laughing.

After the grand lunch the children went to see over the

Palace. 'My word – you're lucky to be able to spend the rest of your hols here, Gussy,' said Jack. 'It's a wonderful place. Not that I'd like to *live* here, of course – but to stay for a few weeks as you'll be able to do – you're jolly lucky!'

'We shall miss you, Gussy,' said Lucy-Ann. 'I suppose we'll be leaving tomorrow, or sometime soon. I'm quite sorry this adventure is over.'

'But it *isn't*,' said Gussy, his face beaming all over. 'It isn't! I have asked my uncle to let me have you here as my guests. You will stay? Or do you not like me well enough? You have so often tizzed me – like when my finger blidded.'

'Oh, Gussy – it doesn't mean we don't like people when we tease them!' said Lucy-Ann. 'Do you *really* mean that your uncle wants us to stay? All of us? I don't want to stay without Bill and Aunt Allie.'

'All of you,' said Gussy, beaming again. 'Kiki and Snoozy too. But not Pedro and the others because they must go with the circus, they say. Then you will stay with me till we go back to school togezzer?'

'We'd love to,' said Jack. 'I could do with a couple of weeks in a Palace. I'll take some pictures back to show the boys. They'll think I'm telling them fairy-tales if I don't!'

Pedro, Ma, Toni and Bingo said goodbye to the five children that evening. They were still wearing their splendid clothes. 'We've been told we can keep them,' said Pedro, grinning. 'I shall fancy myself when I go into the ring to help Toni and Bingo set up their wires now – the Great and Only Pedro the Magnificent.'

He bowed himself almost to the ground. Ma gave him a resounding slap. 'Ha! You will peel potatoes for your old ma tonight!' she said, and laughed loudly. Kiki imitated her and made her laugh all the more.

The children were sorry when the circus folk had gone. They had been such good friends. 'I hope we'll see them sometime again,' said Lucy-Ann. 'I liked them all.'

'You will now come to my uncle and tell him you will stay, plizz?' begged Gussy, who seemed to think they might change their minds. 'And I have to ask him something. You must help me with it.'

He dragged them off to his uncle's room. They all bowed politely. 'Well, Aloysius,' said the King, looking amused. 'Have you persuaded your friends to put up with you and stay for the rest of the holidays?'

'They will stay,' said Gussy. 'And, sir, I have something else to beg of you – BEG of you, sir. These boys, they will tell you it is very, very important. You will grant it to me, sir?'

'I might, as I feel quite pleased with you at the moment,' said his uncle, smiling. 'But tell me what it is first.'

'It is my *hair*,' said Gussy. 'I want it short – snip snip – like Philip's and Jack's. I will not look like a girl, I WILL NOT.'

'You're not supposed to wear it short, Aloysius,' said

his uncle, 'but I know how you feel. I felt the same when I was a Prince and went to school in England. Very well – you shall have it cut short!'

Gussy's face was a study. Nothing in the world could have pleased him more. 'I go tomorrow,' he said. 'I go tomorrow at seven o'clock in the morning. Ha – it will be so short that never will a ribbon sit on it again!'

'Thank you for asking us to stay, Your Majesty,' said Jack, speaking for all the others. 'We shall love it, and it's nice of Gussy to want us.'

'Fussy-Gussy!' cried Kiki, saying quite the wrong thing.

'Fussy-Gussy! Your Majesty! Majesty, Majesty! Send for the doctor. Blow your nose.'

'*Kiki!*' said Jack, shocked.

Kiki looked at the King. She raised her crest to its fullest height, and gave a little bow. 'Your Majesty!' she said. 'God save the King!'

Don't miss . . .

The *River* of adventure

*the next exciting book in Enid Blyton's
thrilling Adventure series*

1

Four miserable invalids

'Poor Polly!' said a small sad voice outside the bedroom door. 'Poor Polly! Blow your nose, poor Polly!'

There was the sound of loud sniffs, and after that came a hacking cough. Then there was a silence, as if the person outside the door was listening to see if there was any answer.

Jack sat up in bed and looked across at Philip in the opposite bed.

'Philip – do you feel you can bear to let Kiki come in? She sounds so miserable.'

Philip nodded. 'All right. So long as she doesn't screech or make too much noise. My head's better, thank goodness!'

Jack got out of bed and went rather unsteadily to the door. He and Philip, and the two girls as well, had had influenza quite badly, and were still feeling rather weak. Philip had had it worst, and hadn't been able to bear Kiki the parrot in the bedroom. She imitated their coughs and sneezes and sniffs, and poor Philip, much as he loved birds and animals, felt as if he could throw slippers and books and anything handy at the puzzled parrot.

Kiki came sidling in at the door, her crest well down. 'Poor thing,' said Jack, and she flew up to his shoulder at once. 'You've never been kept out before, have you? Well, nobody likes your kind of noises when their head is splitting, Kiki, old thing. You nearly drove Philip mad when you gave your imitation of an aeroplane in trouble!'

'Don't!' said Philip, shuddering to think of it. 'I feel as if I'll never laugh at Kiki's noises again.' He coughed and felt for his handkerchief under the pillow.

Kiki coughed too, but very discreetly. Jack smiled. 'It's no good, Kiki,' he said. 'You haven't got the flu, so it's no use pretending you have.'

'Flue, flue, sweep the flue,' said Kiki at once, and gave a small cackle of laughter.

'No, we're not quite ready yet to laugh at your idiotic remarks, Kiki,' said Jack, getting back into bed. 'Can't you produce a nice bedside manner – quiet voice, and sympathetic nods and all that?'

'Poor Polly,' said Kiki, and nestled as close to Jack's neck as she could. She gave a tremendous sigh.

'Don't – not down my neck, please,' said Jack. 'You *are* feeling sorry for yourself, Kiki! Cheer up. We're all better today and our temperatures are down. We'll soon be up and about, and I bet Aunt Allie will be glad. Four wretched invalids must have kept her hands full.'

The door opened cautiously, and Aunt Allie looked in. 'Ah – you're both awake,' she said. 'How do you feel? Would you like some more lime juice?'

'No, thanks,' said Jack. 'I tell you what I suddenly – quite suddenly – feel like, Aunt Allie – and that's a boiled egg with bread-and-butter! It came over me all at once that that was what I wanted more than anything else in the world!'

Aunt Allie laughed. 'Oh – you *are* better then. Do *you* want an egg too, Philip?'

'No, thanks,' said Philip. 'Nothing for me.'

'Poor boy, poor boy,' said Kiki, raising her head to look at Philip. She gave a small cackle.

'Shut up,' said Philip. 'I'm not ready to be laughed at yet, Kiki. You'll be turned out of the room again if you talk too much.'

'Silence, Kiki!' said Jack and gave the parrot a small tap on the beak. She sank down into his neck at once. She didn't mind being silent, if only she were allowed to stay with her beloved Jack.

'How are the two girls?' asked Jack.

'Oh, *much* better,' said Aunt Allie. 'Better than you two are. They are playing a game of cards together. They wanted to know if they could come into your room this evening and talk.'

'I'd like that,' said Jack. 'But Philip wouldn't, would you, Phil?'

'I'll see,' said Philip grumpily. 'I still feel awfully bad-tempered. Sorry.'

'It's all right, Philip,' said his mother. 'You're on the mend – you'll feel yourself tomorrow!'

She was right. By the evening of the next day Philip was very lively, and Kiki was allowed to chatter and sing as much as she liked. She was even allowed to make her noise of an express train racing through a tunnel, which brought Mrs Cunningham up the stairs at once.

'Oh *no*!' she said. 'Not *that* noise in the house, please, Kiki! I can't bear it!'

Dinah looked at her mother, and reached out her hand to her. 'Mother, you've had an awful time looking after the four of us. I'm glad you didn't get the flu too. You look very pale. You don't think you're going to have it, do you?'

'No, of course not,' said her mother. 'I'm only just a bit tired racing up and down the stairs for the four of you. But you'll soon be up and about – and off to school!'

Four groans sounded at once – and then a fifth as Kiki joined in delightedly, adding the biggest groan of the lot.

'School!' said Jack, in disgust. 'Why did you remind us of that, Aunt Allie? Anyway I hate going back after the term's begun – everyone has settled down and knows what's what, and you feel almost like a new boy.'

'You *are* sorry for yourselves!' said Mrs Cunningham, with a laugh. 'Well, go on with your game – but do NOT let Kiki imitate aeroplanes, trains, cars or lawn-mowers.'

'Right,' said Jack, and addressed himself sternly to Kiki. 'Hear that, old thing? Behave yourself – if you can.'

'Mother does look a bit off-colour, doesn't she?' said Philip, dealing out the cards. 'I hope Bill will take her for a holiday when he comes back from wherever he is.'

'Where *is* he? And hasn't anyone heard from him lately?' asked Dinah, picking up her cards.

'Well, you know what old Bill is – always on some secret hush-hush job for the Government,' said Philip. 'I think Mother *always* knows where he is, but nobody else does. He'll pop up out of the blue sooner or later.'

Bill was Mrs Cunningham's husband. He had married her not so very long ago, when she was the widowed Mrs Mannering, and had taken on Dinah and Philip, her own children, and the other two, Jack and Lucy-Ann, who had always looked on her as an aunt. They had no parents of their own. All of them were very fond of the clever, determined Bill, whose job so often took him into danger of all kinds.

'I hope Bill will come back before we return to school,' said Jack. 'We haven't seen him for ages. Let's see – it's almost October now – and he went off into the blue at the beginning of September.'

'Disguised!' said Lucy-Ann, remembering. 'Disguised as an old man, do you remember? I couldn't think who the old, bent fellow was who was sitting with Aunt Allie that night he left. Even his hair was different.'

'He had a wig,' said Jack. 'Buck up, Dinah – it's your turn. Have you got the king or have you not?'

Dinah played her card, and then turned to the radio nearby. 'Let's have the radio on, shall we?' she said. 'I feel as if I'd like to hear it tonight. Philip, can you bear it?'

'Yes,' said Philip. 'Don't pity me any more. I'm as right as rain now. Gosh – when I think how miserable I was I really feel ashamed. I wouldn't have been surprised if I'd burst into tears at any time!'

'You did once,' said Jack, unfeelingly. 'I saw you. You looked most peculiar.'

'Shut up,' said Philip, in a fierce voice. 'And don't tell fibs. Dinah, that set's not tuned properly. Here, let me do it – you're never any good at that sort of thing! Dinah – let *me* do it, I said. Blow you!'

'Aha! Our Philip is quite himself again!' said Jack, seeing one of the familiar brother-and-sister quarrels beginning to spring up once more. 'You've got it, now, Philip – it's bang on the station. Ah – it's a skit on a burglary with John Jordans in it. It should be funny. Let's listen.'

It *was* funny, and Aunt Allie, having a quiet rest downstairs, was pleased to hear sudden roars of laughter upstairs. Then she heard a loud and prolonged whistle and frowned. That tiresome parrot!

But it wasn't Kiki. It was John Jordans in the comical play. He was the policeman, and was blowing his police whistle – pheeeeeeee! Then someone yelled, 'Police! Police!' and the whistle blew again.

'Police, police!' yelled Kiki too, and produced a marvellous imitation of the whistle. 'PHEEEEEEEE! Police! Police! PHEEEEEEEEEEEE!'

'Shut up, Kiki! If you shout and whistle as loudly as that you'll have the *real* police here!' said Jack. 'Oh, my goodness! – I hope Kiki doesn't start doing this police-whistle business. She'll get us into no end of trouble! Kiki – if you shout "Police" *once* more, I'll put you down at the very bottom of the bed.'

Before Kiki could make any reply, a knock came on the bedroom door – a most imperious knock that made them all jump. A loud voice came through the door.

'Who wants the police? They're here. Open in the name of the law!'

The door opened slowly, and the startled children watched in amazement. What did this mean? Had the police really come?

A face came round the door, a smiling face, round and ruddy and twinkling, one that the children knew well and loved.

'BILL!' cried four voices, and the children leapt out of bed at once, and ran to the tall, sturdy man at the door. 'Oh, Bill – you've come back! We never heard you come home. Good old Bill!'

The  of adventure

Something very sinister is happening on the mysterious Isle of Gloom and the children are determined to uncover the truth!

But Philip, Dinah, Lucy-Ann and Jack are not prepared for the dangerous adventure that awaits them in the abandoned copper mines and secret tunnels beneath the sea.

The  of adventure

Why is everyone so afraid of the castle on the hill, and what dark secrets lurk inside its walls?

When flashing lights are seen in a distant tower, Philip, Dinah, Lucy-Ann and Jack decide to investigate – and discover a very sinister plot concealed within its hidden rooms and gloomy underground passages.

The  of adventure

Who are the two strange pilots, and what is the secret treasure hidden in the lonely valley where the children land?

Nothing could be more exciting than a daring night flight on Bill's plane! But Philip, Dinah, Lucy-Ann and Jack soon find themselves flying straight into a truly amazing adventure.

The  of adventure

A mysterious trip to the desolate Northern Isles soon turns into a terrifying adventure when Bill is kidnapped!

Marooned far from the mainland on a deserted coast, Philip, Dinah, Lucy-Ann and Jack find themselves playing a dangerous game with an unknown enemy. Will they escape with Bill and their lives?

The *Mountain*

of adventure

Surely a peaceful holiday in the Welsh mountains will keep the children out of trouble! But the mystery of a rumbling mountain soon has them thirsty for more adventure.

Philip, Dinah, Lucy-Ann and Jack are determined to explore the mountain and uncover its secret, but first they must escape from a pack of ravenous wolves and a mad genius who plans to rule the world!

The
of adventure

An amazing voyage around the beautiful Greek islands
becomes an exciting quest to find the lost treasure of the
Andra!

Philip, Dinah, Lucy-Ann and Jack are plunged into a search
for hidden riches – with some ruthless villains hot on their
trail! Will they find the treasure before it's too late?

The *Circus*
of adventure

Why did Bill have to bring the babyish Gustavus with them on holiday? Jack knows he'll only be trouble . . .

But when Gustavus is kidnapped, along with Philip, Dinah and Lucy-Ann, Jack bravely sets out to rescue them, leading him to a faraway land and the discovery of a plot to kill the King!

The *River* of adventure

A river cruise through ancient desert lands becomes a mysterious adventure when Bill disappears!

While Philip, Dinah, Lucy-Ann and Jack are desperately searching for Bill, they become trapped beneath a forgotten temple where no one has set foot for 7,000 years. What dangers lurk within, and will they ever escape?